TARTAN TITTERS!
The ULTIMATE Scottish Joke Book

TARTAN TITTERS!

The ULTIMATE Scottish Joke Book

Allan Morrison

Black & White Publishing

First published 2008
by Black & White Publishing Ltd
29 Ocean Drive, Edinburgh EH6 6JL

1 3 5 7 9 10 8 6 4 2   08 09 10 11 12

ISBN: 978 1 84502 222 8

Typeset by RefineCatch Limited, Bungay, Suffolk
Printed and bound by Norhaven A/S Denmark

INTRODUCTION

With our buoyant demeanour and outgoing nature, isn't Scottish humour just grand!

Reading this book will produce the cackling sound of Scottish laughter for we Scots have something that sets us apart from other countries . . . the justified reputation of being able to laugh at ourselves. The nation that laughs together can conquer all challenges, as our history proves.

It is a humour that travels well from this epicentre of western civilisation to delight the rest of the world. Our culture is a hard working, living one, with laughter a necessary part of our lives. Remember, girn and grin come from the same derivation.

Jokes add sparkle to life. They help us to learn to laugh at ourselves and the world. They are a powerful antidote to life's cares and woes. A chuckle overrides anxiety, boosts mood and helps lessen emotional pain. They ensure we do not take life too seriously.

Jokes can be a wonderful form of entertainment. They are also a positive, unifying force. Jokes can lift an audience or individual like a breath of fresh air when the subject or going gets tough.

This book of quality Scottish jokes can be used for personal enjoyment or for stories to share with friends and family. It can also enliven and illustrate speeches.

Many Scottish jokes poke fun at our lifestyle, our Parliament, our Health Service, our industries or certain divisions of our population. They range from the traditional to the contemporary.

Scotland is one of the friendliest, most generous nations on earth. We Scots are also an enterprising lot. The humour in this joke book demonstrates this, offering an intimate and vivid picture of the Scottish psyche. The stories that we circulate about ourselves are the stories that define us.

Hopefully the book will be a treasure and joy to read, and much laughter and chuckling will result.

CONTENTS

LADS AND LASSIES!

A very attractive lady asked a waiter to take a note and a double whisky to a kilted Scotsman at the next table. It read, "Please accept this double whisky. If you have seven inches under that kilt then I am in room 142."

The Scotsman sent the whisky back. "Tell her that ah'm no' cuttin' aff three inches, even fur a dram!"

* * *

A wee Scottish couple had just returned from honeymoon. The husband, although deeply in love with his wife, just couldn't wait to go down to the pub and drink with his mates.

"Darling, ah'm jist going out for a wee while."

"And where are you going, my precious love?"

"I'm just going down to the pub, my gorgeous one, for a beer."

His wife said, "Oh, you want a beer, my lovely?" She opened the fridge and showed him a stack of bottles and tins of beer.

The husband didn't know what to say. Then he said. "But listen, sweetheart, at the pub they have salted peanuts and you know how I love them."

"You want salted peanuts, my handsome hunk?" And she opened a kitchen cupboard to show packets of salted peanuts plus a huge variety of potato crisps.

"But, but, my sweetie . . . at the bar there is football talk, swearing and all sorts of bad words."

"Oh, you want bad words, cutie pie? RIGHT, LISTEN YOU PATHETIC LITTLE MAN, SIT DOWN, SHUT YOUR CAKEHOLE, DRINK UP YOUR DAMN BEER AND EAT YOUR BLEEDIN' SALTED PEANUTS BECAUSE YOUR MARRIED ASS AIN'T GOING TO ANY PUB. AND ANOTHER THING . . . YOUR TEAM'S CRAP!"

And they both lived happily ever after.

* * *

"I bet you don't know what day today is, darling?" queried the wife to her husband as he made his way out of the door. The husband was perplexed, but was always a quick thinker.

"Of course I do, my love," he replied. "How could I forget?" With that he got in the car and went off to work.

At 11am the doorbell rang and when the wife opened the door, she was handed a box of roses.

At 1pm the doorbell rang again and there was a delivery of an upmarket box of chocolates.

At 3pm the doorbell once more rang and there was a delivery from a local jewellers of a string of pearls.

When the husband arrived home, he was confident he had managed to recover from what could have been a very bad situation.

"My darling," said his wife. "Roses, chocolates and pearls . . . wonderful. It's the best Saint Andrew's day I've ever had!"

* * *

"Wake up, John. For heavens sake wake up! There's a burglar going through your trouser pockets."

"Och, you two jist fight it oot among yerselves!"

* * *

The wife had spent all day in an Edinburgh beauty salon. When she came home she was anxious for her husband to appraise the results. "How old do you think I look now?" she asked.

"Well, looking at your skin I would say twenty-five. Looking at your hair I would say twenty. Looking at your nails I would . . ."

"Oh, stop it," replied his giggling wife. "You're just flattering me."

"Hey, hang on a wee minute, pet. I hav'nae added it all up yet!"

* * *

Kenny phoned his wife to say he was bringing a work colleague home for dinner. His wife went ballistic. "Listen, the house is a mess, ah huvnae hoovered this week, the bed is not made, the sink is full of dirty dishes, ah'm just oot o' bed an' still in ma dressing gown. Ah huvnae enough food for three people. Anyways, you know we just usually have carry-oots. So, why on earth dae ye want tae bring him here fur a meal?"

"The poor fool is thinkin' o' getting' married!"

* * *

A guest speaker was making a presentation to a Glasgow audience about his travels throughout the Middle East. "Women are treated as second class citizens. Sometimes you see a woman and a donkey hitched up together."

A female voice immediately came from the audience. "That's no' unusual. Ye get that in Glesca aw the time!"

* * *

In the golf club bar John was complaining to his pal Dick about his wife's purchasing of clothes. "And the trouble is that she

3

continually denies all this spending. In fact it's got to the stage that I now call her Narnia."

"That's an unusual pet name. Why do you call her Narnia?" asked Dick.

"Because she's a lying witch with a wardrobe!"

* * *

Hamish was in trouble. He had forgotten his wife's birthday . . . and it was a 'big birthday'. She was really, really angry. "Listen you," she screamed. "If tomorrow morning I don't find a gift outside our garage that goes from zero to umpteen in less than 5 seconds . . . YOUR LIFE WILL BE HELL!"

The following morning Hamish left the house early. When his wife woke she looked out of the window and there was a box, all gift-wrapped, sitting in the middle of the driveway. Quickly she put on her dressing gown and brought the box back into the house. She opened it and found brand new bathroom scales.

After three months the police have yet to find Hamish's body.

* * *

It was the day before he married and one of his friends observed, "Someday you will look back at today as the happiest day of your life."

"But I'm not getting married until tomorrow."

"Aye, ah know that."

* * *

An old Highlander was sued by a woman neighbour for defamation of character.

She charged that he had called her a pig. The old Highlander was found guilty and fined. At the end of the trial he asked the sheriff, "Does this noo mean ah cannae call Mrs MacKinnon a pig?"

The sheriff said that was correct.

"Well, does this mean ah cannae call a pig Mrs MacKinnon?" asked the Highlander.

The sheriff confirmed that he could indeed call a pig Mrs MacKinnon with no fear of legal action.

The Highlander turned and looked at Mrs MacKinnon and said, "Good efternoon to you, Mrs MacKinnon."

* * *

An Edinburgh man came home one day and asked his wife: "If I was, let's say, severely disfigured, would you still love me?"

"Darling, I'll always love you," she calmly replied, as she filed her nails.

"How about if I lost all my limbs, would you still love me then?" he asked nervously.

"Don't worry, darling, I'll always love you," she told him as she painted her nails.

"Well, if I told you I had lost my eighty-five thousand pounds a year job, would you still love me, then?"

The woman looked up at her husband's worried face as she examined her finished nails. "James, I'll always love you. But most of all, I'll really miss you."

* * *

One night a couple in Dundee were in bed when the woman became aware that her husband was touching her.

He started by running his hand across her shoulders down to the small of her back. Then he proceeded to run his hand over her stomach from one side of her waist to the other. He then probed up the inside of her thighs.

By this time the woman was becoming aroused and she squirmed a little to get into a better position. Then the man stopped abruptly and rolled over to his side of the bed.

"Why are you stopping, darling?" she whispered.

He whispered back. "It's okay, pet, I've found the TV remote. Scotsport starts in five minutes."

* * *

Jack went to his doctor for a check up. "You're in great shape for a man of your years," said the doctor. "You're seventy-five and you look like fifty-five. What's your secret?"

"You see, doc," replied Jack, "when I got married my wife and I made a pact. Whenever we had an argument we agreed that my wife would go into the kitchen to cool down and I would go outside to cool down."

"Good idea," commented the doctor. "But how does that explain your excellent health?"

"I put it down to fresh air, doc. For the past fifty years I've mostly been living outdoors!"

* * *

"Darling," said the wife. "Will you still love me when my hair has gone grey?"

"Why shouldn't I? I've loved you through about five different colours so far!"

* * *

The English husband turned to his Scottish wife and observed, "You know, dear, forty years ago we rented a one-bedroomed flat, had no car, no television, no money, just debts, and we slept on a mattress on the floor. But I got to sleep every night with a hot, sexy, good-looking eighteen-year-old. Now we have a lovely four-bedroomed house, two top of the range cars, a king-sized bed, a forty-two inch telly and plenty of dosh, but I'm sleeping with a fifty-eight year old woman."

"Well, darling," said the wife. "Jist you go out and find a hot, sexy, good-looking eighteen year old woman . . . and I'll make sure that once again you will have a rented one-bedroomed flat, no car, no television, no money, just debts, and you will be able to sleep on a mattress on the floor with your dolly bird!"

* * *

The Scot was walking down a street when he heard a voice. "Stop! Stand still! Do not move. If you take one more step a brick will fall on your head and kill you." The Scot stopped and a brick fell right in front of him, smashing on the pavement.

An hour later the chap was just about to cross a road when the voice came again. "Stop! Stand still! Do not move. If you take one more step a bus will run you over." The man stopped and a double-decker bus came careering round a corner barely missing him.

"Where are you?" the man asked looking up to the sky. "Who are you?"

"I am your very own guardian angel," the voice answered.

"So where were you on ma wedding day?"

* * *

Two ladies were talking. "Excuse me, Dorothy, but aren't you wearing your wedding ring on the wrong finger?"

"Aye," said Dorothy. "Ah married the wrang man!"

* * *

A man was drinking in a bar when he suddenly started to sob. The barman asked him what was the matter. The

man said, "You see, my wife and I had a terrible fight and she swore she wouldn't talk to me for a year."

"Don't upset yourself," said the barman. "I'm sure she didn't mean it."

"You don't understand," he said. "Tomorrow's the last day!"

* * *

It was the firm's annual dance. One spotty young lad, who had only just started with the company, decided to ask a particularly pretty lady to dance.

Upon being asked, she gave him the once over, and snootily said, "Sorry, I won't dance with a child."

"Sorry, hen," he replied. "Ah didnae realise ye were pregnant."

* * *

The woman was desperately trying to lose weight. So much so that she taped a photograph of a glamorous topless model onto the fridge.

She lost three stones . . . and her husband put on three stones.

* * *

Two Glasgow women were talking. "Tell me, do you have any, you know, fantasies?"

"Well, actually ah do. Ah'd like to have two men at the wan time."

"Two! At the one time?"

"Aye. Wan cookin' and wan cleanin'!"

* * *

A married couple in Glasgow were trying to live up to the somewhat upmarket lifestyle of a party they were attending in Edinburgh. The conversation turned to

Mozart. "Absolutely brilliant, magnificent, sheer genius," exclaimed one man.

The woman, wanting to join the conversation, remarked casually, "Ah Mozart. You are so right. I love that man. In fact only yesterday I saw him in Glasgow at Buchanan Street bus station getting on a number 42 bus."

There was a sudden hush, and everybody looked at her. Her husband was mortified. He whispered to her, "Right, get your coat and let's get out of here."

As they drove home along the M8 she could see he was fuming. Finally she turned to him and asked, "Are you angry about something?"

"I've never been so embarrassed in all of my life. Imagine saying that you saw Mozart at Buchanan Street bus station getting on a number 42 bus. You are an absolute idiot. The number 42 bus doesnae leave frae Buchanan Street bus station!"

* * *

"See if you really loved me," said the wife to her husband. "You'd get me a mink."

"I would be delighted to do that," replied the husband. "Provided you keep its cage clean."

* * *

The bus driver in Glasgow stopped at a bus stop. On to the bus came the biggest tough he had ever seen. Six feet six, shaven head, tattoos all over his arms and face, and a ring through his nose.

"Fares, please," said the driver.

"Big Tam doesnae pay," grunted the brute and sat down.

The following day at the same bus stop, on came this monster once more.

9

"Fares, please," said the driver nervously.

"Big Tam doesnae pay!"

The next two days were the driver's off days, so he determined he must be a man and somehow stand up to this man mountain. So he spent every waking moment doing press-up, squats, and punching his fist into a bucket of sand.

Feeling much more confident, he stopped his bus on the Monday morning at the same bus stop. On came the frightening monster.

"Fares, please," said the driver.

"Big Tam doesnae pay!" thundered the brute.

"Why does Big Tam not pay?" asked the driver feeling nervous again.

"'Cause Big Tam's goat a free bus pass frae the Scottish Executive!"

* * *

"Listen, Heather, you an' yer husband don't seem tae have a lot in common," observed Sally. "Why on earth did you two get merrit in the first place?"

"It's easy, Sally," replied Heather. "You know how they say opposites attract. Well, he wisnae pregnant but ah wis!"

* * *

Two Scots were talking in a bar in Edinburgh.

"Just to let you know," said one, "I'm thinking of divorcing my wife."

"Why on earth would you want to do that, John?"

"She hasn't spoken to me for over two months."

"Well, ah would think carefully about that, John. There aren't too many of them around."

* * *

In the Glasgow theatre a lady stood up at the interval and shouted, "Is there a doctor in the hoose?"

As a result three men shouted out that they were doctors. "Great," shouted the woman as she got her daughter to stand up. "Any o' youse single an' fancy a date wi' ma wee Margaret?"

* * *

The farmer's wife said to her husband, "Tomorrow is our silver wedding anniversary. I think I'll kill the cockerel and we can have him for a special meal."

"Hold on a minute," replied the farmer. "Why punish that poor bird for something that happened twenty-five years ago?"

* * *

The couple were having a wee tiff. He finally said, "I'll admit I'm wrong if you'll admit I'm right."

"Fair enough," said his wife. "But you go first."

"I'm wrong."

"You're right."

* * *

After the bride's first display of independence, her young husband said reproachfully, "Listen Jeannie, have you forgotten that you promised to obey when we married?"

"No, ah havenae forgotten. But there will be time enough for that when I see some of the worldly goods you promised to endow me with!"

* * *

The Aberdonian bought his wife a beautiful diamond ring for her birthday. His pal observed, "Ah thought she wanted a Mercedes sports car?"

"Aye, she did," he replied. "But where in Scotland am ah going tae find a fake Mercedes?"

* * *

The Scottish lady was on a luxury cruise. At the dining table she attracted a lot of attention due to the enormous diamond ring she wore.

"It's the McGregor Diamond," she told her curious table companions, "and, like the notorious Hope Diamond, it carries a terrible curse."

"What's the curse?" her gaping fellow passengers asked.

"Mr McGregor!"

* * *

The various stages of Scottish women.

At 8, you take her to bed and tell her a story.

At 18, you give her whisky, you tell her a story, and take her to bed.

At 28, you don't need to give her whisky or tell her a story to take her to bed.

At 38, she tells you a story, buys you a whisky, and takes you to bed.

At 48, you take too much whisky, and tell her a story to avoid going to bed.

At 58, you take whisky and stay in bed to avoid her story.

At 68, if you take her to bed, that'll be some story!

At 78, what story? What bed? I'll have the whisky though! And anyway, who are you?

* * *

Trying hard to get on a bus, a woman snapped at the man behind her, "Hey, if you were half a gentleman, you'd help me to get onto this bus."

"Aye, an' if you were half a lady, you wouldn't need any help."

* * *

"What happened when you showed off your engagement ring to the girls in the office," asked the proud mum. "Did they admire it?"

"Admire it, mum! Five of them recognised it."

* * *

Advert in the Personal Column of the *Evening Times*.

'Willie MacGregor. Get in touch immediately. Have news. Bring three rings: engagement, wedding and teething. Love, Heather.'

* * *

"You wouldn't sleep with Carol Smillie for a million pounds, would you darling?" asked the Scotsman's wife as she cuddled into him.

"Don't be daft, woman," he replied. "How could ah save up a million pounds?"

* * *

The train was going from Glasgow to Edinburgh. Three men and a ravishing blonde were all seated together. Soon they were chatting and the conversation turned to eroticism.

The young lady said, "Look, I could do with some money. Tell you what, if you all give me a pound I'll show you my legs."

The men, charmed by this lady, all willingly gave her a pound coin. She pulled up her skirt and gave them a good view of her legs.

"I can see you guys are interested, so if you all give me a fiver I will show you my thighs." Fivers were duly produced and the skirt went all the way up to the top of her legs.

Just then the train was approaching Edinburgh and she said, "Look, guys, if you each give me twenty pounds I'll show you where I was operated on for appendicitis."

The three excited men pulled twenty pound notes from their pockets. The lady turned and pointed in the distance. "There's Edinburgh Infirmary where I had it done."

* * *

"See you and me, Mary," said Jim. "We've been married fur seven years and have never ever agreed on one thing."

"Aye, and yer wrang again. It's been six years."

* * *

"I was in a very generous mood today," said the Edinburgh lady. "I gave twenty pounds to a miserable, old beggar."

"My goodness," replied her friend. "That's a lot of money. What did your husband say?"

"Oh he just said, 'Thank you, dear.'"

* * *

"You know," exclaimed a lady, "you and your wife always look so happy when I see you together. What's your secret?"

"Single beds."

"Single beds?"

"Aye. She sleeps in Glasgow and I sleep in Edinburgh."

* * *

Simon McKelvin from Auchtermuchty was a terrible flirt. Once he started going out with a Siamese twin, but after a while he started seeing her sister behind her back.

* * *

The young chap at Aberdeen University called his mother and announced excitedly that he had just met the girl of his dreams.

"Why don't you send her flowers and on the card invite her for a home-cooked meal at your flat?" recommended his mother.

The following week he called his mother. "Mum," he moaned, "Ah wis totally humiliated. She insisted on washing the dishes."

"And just what's wrong with that?"

"We hadn't started eating yet."

* * *

Robbers broke into a branch of a Scottish bank and ordered all the staff to take off their clothes and lie face down on the floor. A nervous young lady pulled off her clothes but lay on her back.

"Turn over, Wendy," whispered the girl lying beside her. "This is a hold up, no' the office Christmas party."

* * *

The groom carried his new bride over the threshold of their new house.

"Oh, Tom, you are so romantic," trilled his wife.

"Well, pet. Ah thought ah wid just give you a wee lift tae yer work."

* * *

"Will there be anything else you wish, sir?" asked the waiter from the Edinburgh hotel's room service.

"No, thanks, that will be all."

As the waiter turned to leave he noticed a sheer negligee on a chair. "What about your wife, sir. Anything for her?"

"Oh, good idea! Could you get me a postcard and stamp, please."

* * *

A Scot was trying to prove to his wife that women talk more than men. He showed her the results of a study by a Scottish university professor that indicated that men use about twelve thousand words each day, whereas women use twenty-four thousand words.

His wife was not too sure about this and thought about it for a while. Then she said that if it was true, it was only because men never listened, and women had to repeat everything they said. Her husband looked up from his newspaper and said, "Whit?"

* * *

"How wis yer blind date last night?" asked Lucy.

"Absolutely awful. The fella turned up in a 1938 Ford."

"An' what's so terrible aboot that?"

"He bought it new!"

* * *

The husband and wife were taking a course in Gaelic. The teacher asked the man if he thought that he would find learning a new language difficult.

"Nut at all," replied the man. "I'll just need tae learn the first two words of each sentence."

"Just the first two words?"

"Aye, ma wife always finishes aff ma sentences."

* * *

The mournful Scot entered the flower shop shortly after it opened one morning. His red eyes displayed that he was deeply upset.

"Morning, sir. Would it be flowers for a funeral?"

"No, no," replied the Scot. "It's for ma wedding anniversary."

"And when do you want the flowers delivered, sir?" she asked.

"Yesterday."

* * *

The Indian businessman in Paisley got a telegram to say that his mother was ill in Umasahad, in India. So, as he did not like flying and he was uncertain how long he would be in India, he went to the railway station to get a single ticket to Umasahad. "Sorry," said the clerk. "But you'll need to go to Glasgow for that."

In Glasgow the booking clerk said that he couldn't possibly give him a ticket to Umasahad and he would need to go to London.

In London the railway authorities told him they could not issue him with a ticket to Umasahad, but they could give him one to Bombay.

In Bombay the chap managed to purchase a ticket for Umasahad.

Finally he got to the station at Umasahad. The railway station consisted of an old hut, serving the small township of approximately a thousand people.

For four months the businessman cared for his mother, and when she finally recovered from her illness he determined it was time to get back to his business in Paisley.

Entering the old railway hut, he asked the clerk if he could possibly purchase a ticket to Paisley.

The clerk replied, "Certainly, sir. Now would that be Paisley Gilmour Street or Paisley West?"

* * *

A wife was watching the Scottish News on television. "Did you see that?" she said to her husband. "A man in Edinburgh has swapped his wife for a season ticket for Hearts at Tynecastle. Would you do such a thing, darling?"

"Don't be stupid. The season's half over."

* * *

Two Glaswegians in a pub. "So whit did ye dae before ye married wee Sadie?"

"Anything ah wanted!"

* * *

Archie was fishing a salmon river in Scotland when he landed a fifteen pound salmon, a magnificent specimen. Another fisherman came up to him to admire the fish, "What a beauty," he said. "I doubt if even Malcolm McBride himself could have caught such a wonderful fish."

"Was Malcolm McBride a champion fisherman?"

"Oh yes, and a wonderful all-round sportsman too. In fact he was a professional athlete. He was also excellent at DIY. I am useless myself but Malcolm McBride could fix absolutely anything. Apparently he was an energetic man, a wizard in bed. I'm not so hot in that department myself. Never ever forgot his wife's anniversary or birthday, a truly amazing person."

"Was Malcolm McBride a friend of yours?"

"Never met him," said the man.

"Then how come you know so much about him?"

"I married his widow."

* * *

Two guys were talking in a pub in Perth.

"My wife and I had the mother of all rows last Saturday night. She wanted to go to the pictures and I wanted to go to the theatre."

"Wis the film any good?"

* * *

A chap and his date were parked in a dark road ten miles from Glasgow. They were doing what men and women are inclined to do.

Just as things were coming to the boil, the girl said to the chap. "Haud on a wee minute, but ah should have mentioned this. Ah'm actually, as they say, in the business, and ah charge thirty pounds for sex."

The chap opened his wallet, paid up, and then finished the business. Then he sat back in the driver's seat, lit a cigarette, put on the interior light, and started to read his newspaper.

"Hey, why are we no' goin' back tae Glesca?"

"Well, I should have mentioned this before, but I'm a taxi driver and the fare back is forty quid!"

* * *

Two men were talking in a pub in Edinburgh. "You know, women do things in a most inefficient way. For years I watched my wife making breakfast. Three or four trips to the cupboards, three or four trips to the fridge, three or four trips to the kitchen table. So I just said to her, 'Listen, dear, why don't you try to carry several things at the one time'."

"And did it save time?" asked his friend.

"It certainly did. It used to take her twenty minutes to make breakfast. Now I do it in ten."

* * *

A Scottish lady was visiting America and was asked to sing at a Scottish gathering.

She opted to sing, *Flower o' Scotland*, and as she sang she was conscious of an old lady on a front seat quietly weeping.

After the performance the Scot went over to the old lady, gently put her hand on the lady's shoulder, and said, "I assume you are of Scottish descent?"

"No, dear. I'm a singing teacher."

* * *

A young clansman rode into the Highland glen to ask for the Clan Chief's daughter's hand in marriage.

"Before you can marry ma daughter," said the Clan Chief, "you must bring me back the feather from a live golden eagle."

After many months the young man managed to get hold of a golden eagle, remove a feather, and then return to see the Clan Chief.

"Now I have obtained a feather from a live golden eagle may I have the hand of your beautiful daughter in marriage?"

"Before you can marry my daughter," said the Clan Chief, "you must bring me a hair from the head of the English King."

After many, many months, the young clansman manages to sneak into the royal palace in London and cut off a hair from the King's head. He then returns to the glen in Scotland to see the Clan Chief.

"Now I have obtained a hair from the head of the English King may I ask for the hand of your beautiful daughter in marriage?"

"Before you can marry my daughter," replied the Clan Chief, "you must bring me back the crown of Scotland, held under lock and key in Edinburgh Castle."

After many, many, many months and much planning, the young man manages to steal the crown of Scotland and returns to the Clan Chief.

"Now I have obtained the crown of Scotland may I now have the hand of your beautiful daughter in marriage?"

"Aye," said the Clan Chief. "You have carried out ma three tasks. You may now ask for the hand of ma daughter in marriage."

The young man was escorted to see the Chief's daughter.

"Your father, the Clan Chief, has given me permission to ask for your hand in marriage. Will you marry me?"

"Naw. Beat it!"

* * *

"Do you know, Dave, ma wife has the worst memory of anybody I know."

"Forgets everything?"

"Naw. Remembers everything."

* * *

"You've been studying our marriage certificate for over an hour, Willie."

"Aye, ah'm looking for the expiry date!"

* * *

The Japanese soldier had been on a Pacific Island for ten years after the war finished, before he found out that the conflict was over.

Returning to his flat in Tokyo, the door was answered by his wife.

"You dishonourable wife!" he said. "I have been told by neighbour that you have been living with Scottish soldier from city called Glasgow in the distant country of Scotland."

"No' me, Jimmy."

* * *

The Edinburgh husband and wife were all snug in bed. The passion seemed to be heating up. Suddenly the wife stopped and said, "I don't feel like it. I just want you to hold me."

"What!" exclaimed the husband.

"Yes. You must be in tune with my emotional needs as a WOMAN."

The following day they went shopping in Jenners. He had her try on three very expensive outfits, then two pairs of shoes at over two hundred pounds, then a handbag at five hundred pounds, then some diamond earrings at a thousand pounds.

The wife was all excited and said, "Right, I'm ready to go home now. Let's go to the counter and pay."

The husband turned to her and said, "No dear, we are not going to buy all this stuff. I just want you to hold them."

"What!" exclaimed the wife.

"Yes. You must be in tune with my financial needs as a MAN!"

* * *

Two young ladies were talking on an Edinburgh bus. One giggled and confided in her companion. "You know, last week ah lost ma virginity on a bus on this route."

"Did ye check at the depot tae see if onybuddy had handed it in?"

* * *

Two businesswomen opened a small manufacturing plant on the outskirts of Edinburgh. They advertised for staff, the adverts all stating that they would only consider married Scotsmen.

A reporter phoned to enquire why they were discriminating in this way.

The answer the reporter got was that married Scotsmen were used to obeying instructions, accustomed to being shoved around, know how to keep their mouths closed, and don't pout when shouted at!

* * *

The Scottish Executive has brought out a series of evening classes specifically designed for Scottish men. It is an intensive nine week course with a diploma issued at completion.

Week One: 'The Toilet Roll . . . Does it change itself?'

Week Two: 'Is it possible to urinate using the technique of lifting the seat, avoiding the floor, walls and bath?'

Week Three: 'Dirty Dishes – can they levitate and fly into the dishwasher themselves?'

Week Four: 'Loss of Identity – allowing the TV Remote to be used by other people.'

Week Five: 'Learning to Find Things – starting with looking in the right place and not turning the house upside down while shouting.'

Week Six: 'Men's Health – why buying her flowers is not harmful to your health.'

Week Seven: 'Is it genetically impossible to sit quietly while your wife parks?'

Week Eight: 'How to be the ideal shopping companion.'

Week Nine: 'The dishwasher, cooker and oven; what are they and how do they work?'

* * *

Sandy said to Fiona, "Here, my dear, is the engagement ring I promised you."

"But Sandy, this diamond has a flaw in it."

"But Fiona, you won't notice it. We are in love and love is blind."

"Aye, Sandy, but not stone blind!"

* * *

A man went to a psychiatrist. "The problem is I love my wife but she is continually unfaithful to me. She is a beautiful twenty-three-year-old and every night she is in the Thistle Hotel picking up men. She seems to just want sex, sex all the time. She is a nymphomaniac. It's driving me crazy. What can I do?"

"First things first," said the psychiatrist. "Now, where is the Thistle Hotel?"

* * *

The young wife complained to her husband, "You love Rangers more than you love me."

"Maybe so, darling," her husband replied, "but at least I love you more than fishing and golf."

* * *

The ageing Scottish actor was chatting up a young lady at the bar of a Scottish hotel.

"Don't you recognise me, dear?" he asked.

"Not really," she replied.

"But I am quite well known in the cinema," he protested.

"Oh. An' where dae ye usually sit?"

* * *

The long-married couple were going round the Royal Highland Show at Ingliston when they came across a bull in a pen. On the fence a notice said, 'This bull mated over three hundred times last year.'

The wife said, "My goodness. That's nearly every day. He could teach you a thing or two, eh?"

"Really?" sighed her husband. "Let's ask him if it was over three hundred times with the same silly old cow!"

SPORTING SCOTLAND

The lawn bowler was away on business when he got a call on his mobile. "Dad, I'm phoning to let you know that Wee Tam yer Westie has died."

"Oh, no! Not Wee Tam. I loved that wee dug. How did Wee Tam die?"

"Well, dad. You know that kennel you built in the garden? Well, it went on fire, and Wee Tam died."

"Terrible! But tell me, how did the kennel go on fire?"

"It wis the flames aff the garden hut, dad."

"The garden hut went up in flames! How on earth did the garden hut catch fire?"

"It wis frae sparks aff the hoose, dad."

"Sparks aff the hoose? How did oor hoose go on fire?"

"The curtains in the living room set the hoose on fire."

"How on earth did the curtains in the living room go on fire?"

"It wis frae the flames aff the candles."

"Candles? Was there an electricity failure?"

"Naw, dad. They fell aff the coffin."

"A coffin in oor living room! Who's deid?"

"Mum's deid!"

"Mum's deid! How did mum die?"

"Well, ye see dad, she came in late one night and the lights weren't on, and ah thought it wis a burglar. So ah hit her o'er the heid wi wan o' yer new bowls."

SILENCE . . .

"Listen son, see if you've damaged wan o' ma new bowls you're in big trouble!"

* * *

Harry got a kidnap note saying, 'Bring £25,000 to the Road Hole, the 17th, at the Old Course, St Andrews, on Thursday at 11am or you will never see your wife alive again.'

On Thursday he takes a bag containing £25,000 to the Old Course, but doesn't turn up at the Road Hole until three o'clock in the afternoon.

The kidnapper goes spare. "Listen! You are so lucky I waited. I told you eleven o'clock. Another half hour and I would have killed her."

"Sorry about that," said Harry. "But I lost two balls at the third and then my five iron broke at the ninth."

* * *

In a well-known Scottish prison a new warden was getting to know three inmates who shared a cell.

"And what are you in for?" he asked the first one, who just happened to be wearing a Scotland football jersey.

"Two years for attempted bank robbery. The Sheriff said that if I had actually done it I would have got five years."

"And what about you?" asked the warden, turning to the next prisoner who was wearing a Brazilian football jersey.

"I've got five years for attempted murder. The Sheriff

said that it would have been eight years if I had actually killed the swine."

Turning to the final prisoner, who was wearing an English football jersey he asked, "And what are you in for?"

"Fifteen years. You see I didn't have any lights on ma bike. The Sheriff told me that it would have been twenty if it had been dark."

* * *

The dentist was just about to do some drilling. He turned to the female patient and said, "Listen, ah won't charge for this work provided that while I'm doing it you let out piercing screams."

"But you've given me an injection and I surely won't feel any pain."

"Ah know that. But there's a big European match with an early kick-off ah don't want to miss, and there's still a lot of patients in the waiting room."

* * *

The bowler insisted to his future wife that they must marry on a Thursday. "Why a Thursday?" she asked. "Most people are married on a Saturday."

"Well, you see, dear, ah've worked it out that if we marry on a Saturday oor Silver Wedding will fall on a Monday . . . and that's a league night."

* * *

The gamekeeper came upon a man with two buckets of salmon on the banks of a well-known Scottish river.

"Do you have a licence to catch these fish?" he asked.
The man replied, "No, ah dinnae. These are ma ain pet fish."
"Pet fish?"

"Aye, every day ah bring them doon tae the river tae gie them a wee bit o' exercise. So they go for a wee swim, then ah whistle, and they come back an' jump in the buckets."

"I have never heard of anything so ridiculous in my life! Who are you kidding?"

"Look," said the man," "I'll show you how it works."

He then poured the fish into the river.

"Nonsense," said the gamekeeper. "I'm going to book you for taking these fish from this river."

"What fish?"

* * *

Jimmy went into his local job-centre. "Can I help you?" asked the clerk.

"Aye. Ah want a job in a bowling alley."

"Ten-pin?" asked the clerk.

"Naw. Permanent."

* * *

The wee boy was crying his eyes out at Hampden Park. A policeman came up to him and asked, "Lost your daddy?"

The wee fellow sobbed, "Aye, sur."

"What's he like?"

"Scotland, lager and Coronation Street."

* * *

The couple were watching TV. "Listen, Janet," said the husband. "Why do you sit and greet and sniff over a programme on the telly about the imaginary woes of people you have never met?"

"For the same reason," replied his wife, "that you scream and yell when a man you don't know scores a try."

* * *

Two brothers, Angus and Jamie Campbell, had been rambling through Glencoe for a number of hours.

"I'm starving," said Angus.

"So am I," replied Jamie. "Ah could fair murder a McDonalds!"

* * *

The wee Scotland football supporter was sitting in a bar in London. He had just come from Wembley where Scotland had lost to England by a soft penalty. He sat there staring at his drink.

Suddenly a burly English supporter came in, snatched the wee Scotsman's glass and drank it. "So, what are you going to do about that, wee Scotsman?" he crowed.

"Absolutely nothing," replied the wee man despondently. "You see, before ah travelled down fae Scotland ah had lost ma job, then ma wife told me she was leaving me for another man. On the train to London ah had ma wallet stolen. Noo Scotland have lost at Wembley. Then just when ah wis aboot tae end it aw, you came along an' drank the poison."

* * *

"You know I'd move Heaven and Earth to break a hundred," said the golfer as he thrashed around in the rough.

"Try Heaven," said his playing partner. "You've already moved enough earth!"

* * *

The woman was moaning to her friend about her recent fishing trip with her husband.

"Ah did everything wrang again. Ah talked too loudly, ah used the wrang bait, ah reeled in too soon, an' ah caught more fish than he did!"

* * *

The gamekeeper stopped a grouse shooter and asked to see his licence.

"Sir, this is last year's licence," the gamekeeper said.

"I know," said the man, "but I don't need a new licence. I am only shooting at the birds I missed last year."

* * *

The golfer turned to his caddy and said, "This green is awful. The grass looks as though it hasn't been cut for years and the flag is missing. It's the worst golf course I have ever been on in my life!"

"What do you mean golf course?" asked the caddy. "We left that about an hour ago."

* * *

A husband and wife were playing golf at Troon when she suddenly had a heart attack on the eighth green. Just before she passed out she said, "Quick, go and get help."

A short time later the woman came to, looked up, and there was her husband lining up his putt. "In heaven's name, what are you doing?" she gasped. "Did you not go and find a doctor?"

"Yes, dear," replied the husband. "Right now he's on the sixth hole."

"The sixth hole?" exclaimed the astonished wife.

"But don't you worry, dear, the people on the seventh are letting him play through."

* * *

An old lady got into a train at Ayr. In the carriage were two men moaning about their losses that day at Ayr races.

When the old lady got off the train at Paisley, she

gave each of the men a five pound note. "I just love to hear of kindness to animals," she said.

"Sorry, madam," said one of the men, "but I don't understand what you mean?"

"Well, I heard both of you talking about putting your shirts on bleeding horses that were scratched."

* * *

In the middle of a defensive wall at a free kick, Partick Thistle's left back took the ball right in his crotch and passed out with the pain. When he woke up he found himself in Glasgow's Western Infirmary. Though still in pain he asked the doctor, "Doctor, is it bad? Will I be able to play again?"

"Yes, you should be able to," replied the doctor.

"Oh, great. So I can play for my club?" said the man, feeling much relieved.

"Well, just as long as Partick Thistle have a women's team."

* * *

A new ultimate sporting contest has now been started in Scotland. It is called 'English Survivor'.

The contestants all start at Gretna. They drive to Glasgow, then Edinburgh, Dundee, Aberdeen, Inverness, Fort William, Oban and then back to Gretna. The prize is one million pounds.

All contestants must drive a large, white van, with banners sticking to the side that say, 'We love the English Football Team of 1966. We love Jimmy Hill. We love Margaret Thatcher. The Tartan Army is rubbish. England owns North Sea oil. All Scots are wankers.'

The first person to get back to Gretna alive wins the prize.

* * *

The fisherman arrived at the bank of the Tayside fishing river, set up his equipment, and realised he had forgotten his tin of worms. Just then he saw a mole passing by with a worm in its mouth. The fisherman snatched up the mole and stole its worm.

Feeling sorry for the little mole, the fisherman took out his hip flask of whisky, and poured a couple of drops down the mole's throat.

An hour later the fisherman felt a tug at his trouser leg. Looking down he saw the same wee mole with three worms in its mouth!

* * *

A golfer on a small Highland course sliced his shot deep into a ravine surrounded by Scots pine and heather. He took out his eight iron and clambered down the embankment. After many minutes hacking away in the undergrowth, he spotted something glistening under a pile of leaves. As he looked closer he saw it was an eight iron in the hands of a skeleton.

He immediately shouted up to his playing partner, "Willie, I've got a wee problem down here."

"What's the matter?" Willie shouted back.

"Throw me doon a wedge. You cannae get oot o' here wi an eight iron!"

* * *

Sign on the wall of a Scottish golf club.

1. Keep back straight, knees slightly bent, feet shoulder-width apart.
2. Form a loose grip.
3. Must keep your head down. Do not move your head.
4. Avoid a quick back swing.
5. At all costs stay out of the water.
6. Try not to hit anyone.

7.   If you are taking too long, let others go ahead of you.
8.   Do not stand directly in front of others.
9.   Remain quiet while others are preparing.
10. Extra strokes are not allowed.

Now flush urinal

* * *

Three English football fans were bemoaning the fact that their team kept losing.
"I blame the manager," said the first, "if he would get new players then we could be a great side."

"I blame the players," said the second, "if they made more effort they would score more goals."

"I blame my parents," added the third, "if I'd been born in Scotland I'd have supported a decent team."

* * *

The young teuchter had come all the way down from his home in the Highlands to the Borders to have a trial for a rugby side. "Can you tackle?" asked the coach. The teuchter ran into a telegraph pole shattering it to pieces.

"Can you run?" asked the coach. He was timed over a hundred yards and almost broke the Scottish record.

"Finally," asked the coach, "Can you pass a rugby ball?"

"Well, sur. If ah dae manage tae swallow it ah probably wull be able tae pass it."

* * *

A couple of attractive women were playing golf. One lady teed off and watched in horror as her ball headed for a foursome of men playing the next hole.

Her ball hit one of the men, and he immediately clasped his hands together over his crotch, and proceeded to roll around in agony.

The woman rushed to the man's side and said, "I am so sorry, but I am a physiotherapist, let me relieve the pain for you."

So she took his hands away from his crotch, loosened his trousers, and put her hands inside, gently massaging him.

"How does that feel?" she asked.

"Just wonderful. But ma thumb still hurts like hell!"

* * *

Granny MacDougall went into her local bookies every day. She always bet one pound on a horse and every day she won. The bookie asked her how she did it. She told him, "Every day ah just get oot a pin and stick it in the racing section. Ah guess ah'm just lucky."

One day she put on a four-horse accumulator, again betting one pound. All four horses won their races and she won almost five hundred pounds.

The bookie asked her how she had managed to select the winners. She replied, "Ah couldna find ma pin so ah jist used a fork!"

* * *

A man and his dog went into a pub in Falkirk. "Sorry," said the barman, "but we don't allow dogs in this pub."

"But," protested the man, "this is no ordinary dog. This is a talking dog."

"Utter nonsense!" replied the barman.

"Let me prove it to you," said the man. "Now, Rover, what do you call the outside of a tree?"

"Bark!"

"There you are," said the man. "You see, he really can talk."

"Listen. Out! Both of you. You cannae fool me with this talking dog stupidity."

"Let me have another go," said the chap. "Rover, who was Scotland's goalkeeper in the World Cup finals in 1982?"

"Rough!"

"Right! That's it," said the barman. "I've had enough of this." And the man and his dog were shown the door.

Outside, the dog turned to the man and said, "Maybe it wasn't Alan Rough. Maybe it was Andy Goram."

* * *

A Scot turned up at Old Trafford to see Manchester United and was told that seats were £45, £35 and £30, and programmes £5.

"Aye, ok," he said cheerfully, "ah'll jist sit on a programme."

* * *

Einstein went to heaven and had to share his mansion with three Scots.

"What's your IQ?" he asked the first.

"It's 145," replied the Scot.

"Great. We can discuss my Theory of Relativity," replied Einstein.

"And yours?" he asked the second Scot.

"It's 120," came the reply.

"Good. We can discuss new Scottish films, plays and books."

He turned to the third. "And what about you?"

"It's just 79," came the sheepish reply.

"So, how's Forfar Athletic doing?"

* * *

A man had stopped in the street to pay his respects to a passing funeral. He couldn't help but see that a fishing rod and basket were sitting on top of the coffin.

He turned to the chap standing beside him and observed, "Must have been a keen fisherman, eh?"

"Still is," came the reply. "He's off to a fishing competition after they bury his wife."

* * *

A golfer was just about to tee off at Gleneagles when he felt a tap on the shoulder. A man handed him a piece of paper on which was scrawled, 'I have a bad throat and have lóst my voice. I have a doctor's appointment in three hours time, can I play through, please?'

"Certainly not. I've already had to wait half-an-hour to get started today!" replied the golfer angrily.

So the golfer played, was on the green in one shot, was just about to putt when he was hit on the head by a ball, knocking him out.

When he came round he looked up and there was the guy with the sore throat holding up 4 fingers.

* * *

The Clydebank punter was into horse racing in a big way. The night before the Grand National he had a dream about bread. The next day in the bookies he saw that a horse called Pan Loaf was favourite. He went to the bank, got a loan, and put five thousand pounds on Pan Loaf.

At the end of the day he went back to the bookies and asked if the favourite had won the race. "Naw," said the bookie. "It wis an outsider that won."

* * *

In a pub in Glasgow a punter asked his friend, "Hey, Jimmy, how would you like to run in a charity marathon?"

"Piss aff, ya wally. Ah huvnae run fur years. Anyways,

ah smoke forty a day and ah have tae stop fur a rest goin' up stairs."

"Well, it's a marathon fur blind, handicapped people."

"Hey, hoad on," replied Jimmy. "Ah could win that!"

RELIGION

The Sunday school teacher went out on a date. At the restaurant her date asked, "Would you like a beer?"

She replied, "What would my Sunday school children say if I had a beer?"

Her date said, "I need to step outside to have a fag. Do you want a cigarette, too?"

She replied, "What would my Sunday school children say if I smoked?"

Afterwards her date asked if she would like to come back to his place. She agreed.

The following morning as she was putting on her clothes, he asked, "And what would your Sunday school children say now?"

She replied, "Och, I'd just tell them you don't have to drink and smoke to have a good time."

* * *

It was the General Assembly in Edinburgh and a well-known restaurant was full of ministers.

One of the waitresses rushed up to the owner. "Heavens, I've just found out that the first course of watermelon was spiked with vodka. I bet it wis that wee Celtic supporter in the kitchen who fancies himsel as a bit o' a joker."

"Oh no, this is a disaster. And what did the ministers say?"

"Nothing! They're aw too busy slipping the seeds intae their pockets."

* * *

"Now, Tommy," said the Sunday school teacher. "I want you to tell me the Ten Commandments. And to make it easy for you, you can do it in any order."

"Right," said Tommy. "Number eight, number four, number ten . . ."

* * *

An old lady went into her post office to buy stamps for her Christmas cards.

"What denominations?" asked the clerk.

"Let me see now," replied the old lady. "You had better give me 20 Presbyterian, 20 Catholic, 15 Baptists and 5 Wee Frees."

* * *

Four wee boys always played together in the school playground. Unfortunately they couldn't get anyone else to play with them. One of the boys reckoned it was because all the other boys went to church, but they didn't. As such, none of them had been baptised.

The following day at playtime they approached the jannie. "Excuse us, jannie, but nobody else will play with us and we need to be baptised."

"Nae problem," replied the jannie, a glint in his eye.

So he took them into the boys' toilets and dunked their little heads in the w.c., one at a time. Then he said, "There you are boys, you're all baptised."

When they got into the playground one of them asked, "What religion are we now?"

The oldest one said, "Well, we're no' kaflic cause they pour the water on ye."

The second wee boy said, "Well, we're no' baptis cause they dunk all of you under the water."

The third wee boy said, "We're no' Church o' Scotland cause they just sprinkle the water oan ye."

The youngest one said, "Did ye no' smell that water? We must be Pisscopalians."

* * *

The Sunday school teacher asked the wee boy: "Do you know who built the ark?"

"No, ah . . . don't."

"Correct!"

* * *

The sermon was all about achieving inner peace. The congregation in the small Highland town listened intently. The minister proclaimed that one of the best ways to find inner peace was to finish off all the things you have already started.

Taking heed of the sermon an old Highlander went home determined to find inner peace. So he finished off . . . a bottle of Laphroaig, a bottle of Glenfiddich, a bottle of Macallan, a bottle of Talisker . . .

* * *

One day a minister was walking down a street in Dundee. He saw a wee boy on the front porch of a house trying to reach the doorbell. The boy was standing on tiptoes, then jumping up and down, but he still couldn't reach the bell.

The minister went over and said, "Let me help, son," and rang the bell.

"Now what?" asked the minister.

"Run like hell!" screamed the wee boy.

* * *

A fisherman suddenly began attending church faithfully on Sunday mornings instead of going fishing.

The minister was very pleased and said to him, "How nice to see you at our service along with your good wife."

"Well, meenister," said the fisherman, "it's a matter of choice. On balance I'd rather hear your sermon than hers."

* * *

A man visited a church manse and asked to see the minister, a person with a reputation for charity and good works.

In the minister's study the man stood, wearing a sad, mournful face.

"Meenister, I am here to draw your attention to the terrible plight of a poor family in your parish. There is no husband, six young children and the mother is ill. They have no money whatsoever, and are just about to be turned out into the street unless someone pays their rent of one hundred pounds."

"How terrible," exclaimed the minister. "Of course they shall have it. Just let me get my chequebook and go and see them right now. Are you a friend of this poor family?"

"No, meenister. I'm the landlord."

* * *

Old Jock, the farm labourer, whose job over the last fifty years had been mucking out the byre, finally decided to visit a church as he was getting near his end.

Later he was telling his friend Willie about his visit.

"Ah left ma horse and cart ootside in the paddock," he said.

"Ye mean the car park," corrected Willie.

"Then ah was met by a mannie at the door."

"That would be an usher," corrected Willie.

"Well, the usher led me doon a path."

"You mean the aisle," said Willie.

"Then he put me in a stall and told me tae sit there."

"Pew," Willie retorted.

"Aye," recalled Jock. "That's whit the wifie said when ah sat doon beside her."

* * *

God, as we all know, is Scottish.

When he was making the world, he made darkness, then he made light. Then he sat down. "Are you all right, God?" asked an angel.

"Actually ah'm a bit knackered. Ah think ah'll call it a day!"

* * *

Two weeks after her wedding, Linda called the Priest.

"Father," she sobbed, "Tam and I had a dreadful fight last night."

"Now calm down, Linda," said the Priest, "it's not half as bad as you think. Every married couple have their first fight."

"Ah know that, Father. But whit am a gonnie dae wi' the body?"

* * *

One Sunday afternoon, a young lady was out for a stroll on the Island of Skye. As she passed by a small wood she heard cries of distress, and there was a parachutist trapped on the branches of a tree.

"Help, help," he cried.

"What are you doing up there? What happened?"

"I was doing a parachute jump and the blooming thing didn't open."

"Ah'm no' surprised," she replied. "Nothing opens around here on the Sabbath."

* * *

The minister in his Sunday sermon spoke on 'forgiving your enemies'. He then asked the congregation how many were willing to forgive their enemies? About half raised their hands.

Not satisfied, he spoke for another ten minutes then repeated his question. This time about three quarters of the congregation raised their hands. Still not satisfied he went on for another ten minutes. The congregation, with Sunday lunch on their minds, all now raised their hands, with the exception of a sweet elderly lady, Miss McDuff, seated at the back.

"Miss McDuff, why are you not prepared to forgive your enemies?" asked the minister.

"I don't have any enemies, meenister."

"That is wonderful for a person who has lived so long as yourself. How old are you Miss McDuff?"

"Ninety-three, meenister."

"Miss McDuff, you are an example to us all. Please come down to the front and tell the congregation how a good Christian person can live so long and not have any enemies."

The old lady slowly tottered to the front, before standing and addressing the congregation.

"It's easy. Ah've outlived the buggers!"

* * *

The church roof was needing attention, and it was agreed that the treasurer would visit all the church members for donations.

About a week later the minister met the treasurer in

the street. The treasurer was having difficulty in standing.

"Heavens, man," exclaimed the minister, "why are you in such a state?"

"Well, meenister, all of the members insisted on giving me a wee dram after they had given me a donation."

"Glory be," said the minister in despair, "are there no teetotallers in my congregation?"

"Aye," said the treasurer. "But ah wrote tae them."

* * *

The small boy was in church for the first time and watched as the ushers passed around the offering plate.

When they came near his pew, the boy said loudly,

"Don't pay for me, dad, I'm under five."

* * *

The priest was talking to little Mary of his parish.

"I understand from your mummy that God is sending you a little baby brother or sister."

"Yes. And my Daddy says that God alone knows where the money is going to come from."

* * *

The phone in the church manse rang and the minister's wife answered it.

"Can ah speak tae the 'heid hog at the trough'?" said a man's voice.

She haughtily replied. "Well, if you mean the minister then you may call him Reverend, but certainly not address him as the 'heid hog at the trough'.

The voice replied, "Actually ah wis phoning up tae ask where ah should send ma cheque fur fifty thousand pounds fur his steeple fund?"

The minister's wife quickly replied, "You're in luck. The big fat pig just walked in!"

* * *

The old lady was shaking hands with the minister after the Sunday service.

"Ah've goat tae tell ye, minister. Every sermon ye preach is better than the next one."

* * *

It was holiday time, and a priest went to fill his car with petrol, but there was quite a queue of cars ahead of him at the petrol station. Eventually, as he was paying for his petrol, the attendant said to him, "Sorry, Father, but everybody seems to wait till the last minute to get ready for a long journey."

"Aye," said the priest, "it's the same in my business."

* * *

The minister's six-year-old daughter was somewhat stubborn and had been naughty during the week, so her mother decided that as a punishment she couldn't go to the Sunday School Picnic on the Saturday.

When Saturday came her mother felt that perhaps she had been somewhat harsh and changed her mind.

"Listen, dear," she said to her daughter. "I've changed my mind. You can go to the picnic."

"Oh, no!" replied the child.

"But I thought you would be happy to go?" said the mother.

"It's too late," the little girl replied. "I've already prayed for rain!"

* * *

It was the banker's first time in prison and he was allocated a cell to share with a huge brute of a man.

"Ah'm in for a white collar crime, too," the man said.

"Oh really," replied the banker with great relief.

"Aye, ah strangled ma minister!"

* * *

Gerry went to see his local priest. "Father you need to urgently help me. My wife is putting poison in my tea."

"No, no, my son," said the priest. "I am sure you are mistaken. There is bound to be a simple explanation for your fears. You stay here and I'll pop round to your house to see her and get the whole thing sorted out."

An hour later the priest came back. "Well, what can I do, Father?" asked Gerry.

"Listen, my son, if I were you I'd drink the tea."

* * *

It was Sunday morning in a kirk on the Scottish Borders. The minister had thought of a new idea. He asked if anybody wished to come up to the front, and let the congregation know of any situation that required prayer.

A young woman duly stepped up to the microphone and spoke. "I want to tell you about the awful accident that happened to my husband, Fraser. A month ago he was playing rugby and was badly injured in a scrum. He was rushed to hospital in a critical condition but all he suffered was a broken scrotum."

There was a gasp of horror from the congregation. All the men writhed in their pews. "Fraser has been in terrible pain all month. He has trouble breathing and swallowing his food. He can hardly lift anything and cannot go to work at present. He cannot cuddle our children, and worst of all we cannot have an intimate relationship. I would ask that the congregation pray for Fraser and his broken scrotum."

A murmur went round the congregation as they all sympathised with the situation. Many of the men had gone white.

Then, as the murmuring died down, a lone, kilted figure stood up and worked his way slowly, clearly in much suffering, to the front. He painfully adjusted the microphone to his height, then spoke.

"My name is Fraser, and I have only one word to say now that you have heard my wife. That word is STERNUM!"

* * *

The minister recognised the man standing outside the church as someone he had married just a few weeks previously.

"Excuse me, meenister," said the young man, "but do you think that a man should profit from mistakes?"

"No, I do not," said the minister.

"Then, could you give me back the fifty pounds I paid you to marry me?"

* * *

The minister rose to address the congregation. "I am saddened to say that there is a certain man among us who is cavorting with another man's wife. Unless he puts twenty pounds in the collection today his name will be read out from the pulpit."

When the treasurer later counted the collection, there were seventeen twenty pound notes, plus a fiver with a note attached that said, 'You'll get the other fifteen on pay-day.'

* * *

The Bishop instructed his priests that they must be innovative. Congregations were falling. Modern methods must be considered.

However two months later the bishop had cause to phone one of his priests.

"Father Michael, your idea of a 24 hour drive through confessional is wonderful. Shift workers can use the service as they go to or come back from work. However I would like you to consider one small change."

"And what would that be, Bishop?" asked Father Michael.

"It's regarding that flashing neon sign. It certainly is effective and catches the eye. But it has to go, I'm afraid. 'Toot and tell or go to hell' is just a wee bit over the top!"

* * *

The minister needed a lawn mower, but couldn't afford a new one. He saw an advert in the local paper advertising a second hand one at thirty pounds. When he got to the house of the man who was selling the lawnmower, there was the man mowing his lawn with the machine. The minister, seeing the machine worked, gave the man thirty pounds and put the mower in the back of his car.

Once home, he thought he would try it out immediately. However, regardless of the number of times he pulled the starter rope the lawnmower refused to start.

In desperation he phoned the previous owner. "I can't get the mower to start. Can you tell me what to do?"

"Aye."

"Well, what do I do?"

"You've got to curse at it."

"Curse at it? Listen to me. I am a minister. I have been a minister for over twenty years. If I ever did curse, and I am not saying I ever did, I've now forgotten how to do it after all these years."

"Listen, meenister. You jist keep pulling on that rope and it'll all come back tae ye."

* * *

The minister married a couple. The bride had on a veil and he couldn't see her face. After the completion of the ceremony, the man asked, "How much do I owe you, meenister?"

"There is no charge," replied the minister.

"But I want to show my appreciation," insisted the groom, and he gave the minister fifty pounds. The bride then pulled off her veil. The minister gave the man forty-five pounds change.

* * *

A man went to a clairvoyant to try to contact his dead wife. The clairvoyant seated the man at a table then asked him, "What was your wife's name and did she have an occupation?"

"Her name wis Agnes an' she was a waitress."

The clairvoyant closed her eyes and cried, "Agnes, Agnes, if you can hear me make yourself known."

A distant voice was then heard. "Ah cannae. It's no' ma table."

* * *

Father Murphy was walking down the street when he passed one of his parishioners. "Good morning, Father, I see you got out of the wrong side of the bed this morning."

Father Murphy was surprised by the remark but walked on. Soon he passed one of his altar boys. "Good, morning, Father, I see you got out of the wrong side of the bed this morning."

Again he was surprised but he continued on to his appointment with the Monsignor. "Good morning, Father," said the Monsignor. "I see you got out of the wrong side of the bed this morning."

"Funnily enough," replied the priest, "you're the third person to tell me that this morning. Do I look grumpy or what?"

"No, you're wearing your housekeeper's shoes."

* * *

Two wee Catholic boys joined their Protestant pals on a Church of Scotland Sunday School Picnic.

During the traditional races and competitions the wee Catholic boys won everything.

At the end of the day the bus home was held up because the two Catholic boys were missing. The minister went to find them and eventually he came back to the bus with them. He explained to his wife, "I found them in the gents' toilet seeing who could pee the highest. When I saw this I was so angry I hit the roof." "Thank heavens we won at something!" replied his wife.

* * *

The minister was shaking hands at the door of the church after the Sunday morning service.

A man shook hands with him and said, "Meenister, your sermon today made me think of the peace and mercy of God, and the milk of his word."

The minister was flattered and asked the man how his sermon had encouraged such thoughts.

The man replied, "Your sermon passed all understanding, endured forever, and should have been condensed."

FAMILY LIFE

The Scottish father of six children won a toy in a raffle at work. He got all his children together in the living room to ask which one should get the toy.

"Who is the most obedient?" he asked. "Who never, ever talks back to mummy? Who does everything she says?"

"Okay, dad," they replied in unison. "You win!"

* * *

A woman who lived in a tenement was busy washing her windows when she lost her balance and landed in an open wheely-bin below.

A passing tourist looked, observed and shrugged his shoulders before saying, "These Scottish people sure are wasteful with their recycling. That woman looks good for another ten years at least!"

* * *

Two men were standing outside Linn Crematorium in Glasgow. They had just been at the funeral of their old friend William.

"Aye, William was a good, good man. Always popular was William. I think the reason he lived so long was that he was a vegetarian."

"Yer right," replied the other, "there was certainly a big turn up at the funeral."

* * *

Two married ladies, Heather and Janette, were talking. "I have got to be really, really careful not to get pregnant," said Heather.

"But I thought your husband had a vasectomy?" replied Janette.

"That's right," said Heather, "and that's the reason why I need to be really, really careful."

* * *

Jamie was at the doctor for a check up.

"So, how many children do you have now, Jamie?" asked the doctor.

"I've got twelve, doctor. Not a bad number for a life's work, eh?"

"It's about time you thought about your wife, Jamie. She's getting on, you know. Any more children might kill her."

"Don't you worry, doc. We'll not have any more. If she has any more I'll go hang masel'!"

Three months later Jamie's wife told him she was pregnant again. So while she was out one day he went into the garage, and slung a rope round one of the beams. As he was standing on a chair with the rope around his neck a thought entered his head which made him quickly remove the rope.

"Haud on a wee minute," he said to himself. "Whit if ah'm hanging the wrang man!"

* * *

The door-to-door salesman was going from door to door in a Glasgow tenement. "Are your parents in?" he asked the little girl who had answered the door.

"They was but they's oot noo."

"Good grief, little girl. Where's your grammar?"

"In the kitchen washin' the dishes."

* * *

Two Scots were talking. "Ma favourite uncle wis ma uncle Jimmy. Took me tae a' the matches, taught me tae swim, taught me tae ride a bike. The trouble is ah haven't spoken to him fur nearly ten years, and ah feel so guilty."

"Has he just passed away?"

"Naw, he's jist won the Lottery!"

* * *

The supermarket was busy and the mother had her three-year-old daughter sitting at the front of the trolley. Suddenly the wee girl started to cry and the woman said, "Now, Elizabeth, we only have another half of the store to do and then we can go home."

When they reached the vegetable aisles the wee girl started to howl and the mother said, "There, there, Elizabeth, don't cry. We only have to visit the bakery and then we can go home."

At the checkout the wee girl started to scream and shout and the mother gently said, "Elizabeth. We will have paid in five minutes, then out to the car park, and in ten minutes we will be back home."

As they were leaving the store a woman said to the mother, "I couldn't help but hear how you talked to your little daughter, Elizabeth, to calm her down."

The woman said, "My daughter's name is Katie. I'm Elizabeth."

* * *

Sandra and Willie were having a meal with a couple they hadn't seen for a number of years. Over the meal the couples took turns in catching up on events.

"Soon after we got married," said Willie, "we got a wee

chubby creature with cute bow legs, very little hair and no teeth."

"Oh, marvellous. You've had a baby," said the other husband.

"Naw, naw," explained Willie. "Sandra's mother moved in wi' us."

* * *

"Ah there's nothing like getting up at five in the morning," said Kenneth, "and having a half-mile swim in the loch followed by a five mile run before breakfast."

"And how long have you been doing this?" asked his friend.

"Ah start tomorrow."

* * *

The Glasgow lady went to the dentist and settled down in the chair.

"Comfy?" asked the dentist.

"Govan," came the reply.

* * *

In Morningside a woman's small daughter picked up something from the pavement, and was just about to put it in her mouth when her mother said, "No! You do not eat anything that's been on the ground. It is dirty and probably has germs on it."

"Mummy," said the little girl, "you really are so clever. How do you know everything?"

"Listen dear," replied the mother. "All mummies know this kind of information. It's part of the 'mummy test'. If you don't know this kind of stuff they don't let you be a mummy."

"Mummy, if you don't pass the 'mummy test' what happens to you?"

"You become a daddy!"

* * *

The wee farm lad was milking a cow in a field when a bull came charging towards him. As horrified onlookers watched, the wee lad calmly continued his milking.

To everyone's surprise the bull stopped a few inches from the boy, sniffed and turned away.

"Were you not afraid, son?" asked one of the onlookers.

"Naw, naw," the boy replied. "Ah knew this coo was his mother-in-law!"

* * *

A beautiful English woman got into the lift on the ground floor of an Edinburgh department store. She was smelling of expensive perfume. Turning to an old Scots woman in the lift she said, "Giorgio, £120 an ounce."

Another young and beautiful English woman got into the lift, also smelling of exotic perfume. She arrogantly turned to the old Scots woman in the lift and said, "Chanel No.5. £150 an ounce."

The lift stopped on the next floor and just as the old Scots woman was about to leave the lift, she looked both of the other women in the eye, turned, bent over, farted, and said, "Haggis. 85 pence a pound!"

* * *

"Aren't you a twin?" asked Angela.

"Aye," replied Patricia.

"Can they tell you apart?"

"Aye."

"How?"

"Oor Malcolm has a moustache."

* * *

A Polish immigrant in Dundee went to have his eyes tested at a local opticians. "Please read this chart," asked the optician.

'ZXCIWNKLARAC'.

"Can you read it?" asked the optician.

"Read it?" the Pole replied. "Sure, it's ma cousin who lives in Inverness!"

* * *

The interviewer stopped a lady in the street. "Excuse me madam, but I wonder if you wouldn't mind answering a few intimate questions for this survey?"

"It depends how intimate they are," she replied.

"Well, what do you think of mutual orgasm?"

"Nothing. We're with Standard Life."

* * *

The Scot was on the train from Inverness to London. Just after the train reached the border, the man started to whisper to himself, and then laughed. Sometimes he would raise his hand and stop talking, then start again.

The person opposite him in the carriage eventually could no longer contain himself and asked, "Sorry to bother you, but is anything wrong?"

"No," replied the Scot. "It's just that I get so sad leaving Scotland that I cheer myself up by telling myself jokes."

"And why do you raise your hand now and again?"

"Oh, I only do that to stop myself if I've heard the joke before."

* * *

An Aberdonian went into an antiques shop and asked, "How much for the set of antlers?"

"Two hundred quid," replied the assistant.

"That's affa deer," came the response.

* * *

Sign above the bar in a Glasgow pub.
Telephone Answering Service Costs.

"No' here."	**50p**
"Jist left."	**£1.50**
"On his way hame."	**£2.00**
"Huvnae seen him since yesterday."	**£2.50**
"He's no' been in aw week."	**£3.00**
"Never heard o' him."	**£5.00**

* * *

"Whit happened tae you?" asked the hospital visitor to the heavily bandaged Glaswegian sitting up in bed.

"Well, it was the September weekend and we all went down to Blackpool. We all went on the big dipper, The Big One. As we came to the very top of the highest loop I noticed a wee sign by the side o' the track.

"I tried to read it, but it was awful wee and I couldn't make out the words. So, we went round again. But it went so quickly that I still couldn't make it out.

"By now I was really determined tae read the wee notice so we went round again and this time when we reached the top I stood up tae read it better."

"And did you manage tae read the sign this time?" asked the visitor.

"Aye, it said 'Remain seated at all times'."

* * *

The wife told her husband that he would need to cut back on his spending. They now had three children and

he could not go on drinking whisky every night. So he stopped.

A few weeks later he found a receipt for two hundred pounds for cosmetics and beauty treatment. So he challenged his wife.

"Listen, pet. I've given up my whisky and it looks like you haven't given up anything. Why don't you give up make-up?"

She told him. "I buy that make-up for you. It's so I can look my best for you."

"Hell's bells," he replied. "That wis what the whisky was for."

* * *

Wee Jeanie was having a heart to heart talk with her mother.

"Mum, if I get married will I get a husband something like dad?"

"Yes, pet."

"Mum, if I don't get married will I be a crabbit old maid something like auntie Mary?"

"Yes, pet."

"Mum, sure Scotland's a hard place for us women, isn't it?"

* * *

One morning at breakfast, a mother gently broke it to her seven-year-old son that Laddie, their Labrador, had unfortunately died during the night.

Instead of the expected floods of tears, and broken heart, there was a quiet acceptance, and he duly went off to school with his usual kiss and hug.

On his return from school the first thing he asked was, "Where's Laddie?" His mother told him again that Laddie had died. There followed a dreadful scene of tears and sobs.

Eventually she asked why he hadn't been sad in the morning. He replied, "Ah thought you said Daddy!"

* * *

The mother didn't know how to control her five-year-old son. Every person the wee boy met, he went up to them and started punching.

Eventually she took him to a top Scottish psychologist. Immediately the boy was introduced to the psychologist the lad started punching him.

The psychologist bent down and whispered in his ear. The boy ran back to his mother.

"Oh, you've cured him," cried the delighted mother. "What did you say to him?"

"Ah just told him if he ever did that again to anyone, I'd come round to his house and smash his face in!"

* * *

"It's God who has given me such a large family," boasted the Scot.

"How's that?"

"Well, if He didn't want me to have any more children then He wouldn't let me drink on Saturday nights."

* * *

"Did Willie bring you home last night?" the father asked his teenage daughter.

"Yes, sorry if we were late, dad. Did the noise disturb you?"

"No, dear, it wisnae the noise. It was the silence!"

* * *

An Aberdeen couple are just about to go out for dinner.

"Darling," says the wife. "Should I wear my Gucci outfit or the new top range one from Marks?"

"You look stunning in both," replied the husband.

"Darling, should I wear my Cartier watch or the Rolex?" asked the wife.

"Both are just lovely," replied the husband.

"Darling, should I wear my diamond necklace or the real mother-of-pearl one?"

The husband sighs and looks at his watch. "Listen, dearest, if we don't leave soon they will have run out of Big Macs."

* * *

It was a particularly horrific crime, and the judge could not refrain from saying so to the defendant.

"You have pled guilty to the dreadful crime of throwing your mother-in-law out of the window of a twelfth floor flat in your multi-storey building."

"Sorry, your worship, but ah did it without thinking."

"That's no excuse whatsoever. What if someone had been passing underneath at the time?"

* * *

Wee Jimmy was saying his prayers.

"Please God make Glasgow the capital of Scotland. Please God make Glasgow the capital of Scotland. Please God make . . ."

"Why do you want God to make Glasgow the capital of Scotland?" asked his mother.

"Because that's what I put down in my geography exam today."

* * *

Two Highlanders were playing poker in a wee bothie in their glen.

One smiled happily and said, "Ah win!"

"Whit have ye goat?" asked the other.

"Four aces!"

"Ah can beat that," said the other fellow.

"Ye cannae beat that. No way! Whit have you goat?"

"Two sevens an' ma claymore."

"Hey, how come you're always so lucky?"

* * *

A Scot answered the doorbell. Outside was a plumber.

"Are you Mister McLeod?" asked the plumber.

"No," replied the man. "My name is Adamson. The McLeods moved out of here three months ago."

"Typical," fumed the plumber. "Phone you up and tell you it's an emergency, then move away to another address!"

* * *

Two women were talking. Said one, "My small boy sleeps right through the night. Doesn't waken till seven-thirty each morning. Does your boy sleep right through the night?"

"No, ma boy is inclined to wake up in the wee, wee hours of the morning."

* * *

"Dad, why do they call Scots the 'mither-tongue'?" the wee chap asked his father.

"Because fathers seldom get a chance to use it, son!"

* * *

A young chap went to a séance. The medium in charge asked if there was anybody that someone in the audience would like to talk to.

"Can ah speak to ma granny?" requested the young man.

The medium duly went into a trance before announcing. "Right, your granny is standing by to answer any question you may have."

"Granny," asked the chap, "what are you doing there? You're no' deid yet!"

* * *

The Scot was in seeing his doctor for his annual check-up.

"You're in good shape for your age," the doctor told him. "Now, is there anything else you would like to discuss?"

"Well," said the man, "I was thinking of having a vasectomy."

"That's a big decision," the doctor replied. "Have you talked it over with your family?"

"Aye," said the man. "They're in favour, seventeen to one."

* * *

Willie burst into the kitchen howling and crying. "What's the matter, son?" asked his mother. "Ah thought you were out fishing with dad?"

"Ah was, mum," he said, "and dad hooked this huge salmon, the biggest fish he'd ever seen. He reeled it in after an hour or so but just before he landed it, the line broke, he fell into the water, and the fish got away."

"Come on now, Willie. What's a big boy like you crying about a thing like that for? You should just have laughed it off."

"But that's just what ah did, mum."

* * *

"Mummy, how old are you?"
"Thirty-nine, and holding, son."
"Mummy, how old would you be if you let go?"

* * *

Two chaps were talking at the nineteenth hole at their local golf course.

"Last night my wife dreamed she was married to a millionaire."

"You're lucky," said the other. "My wife thinks that during the day!"

* * *

The Scot was showing a friend around his garden. Eventually he showed him into the garden shed, and there was a bum sticking out above the concrete floor.

Surprised and shocked the man asked, "What in the name of the wee man is that?"

"Och," came the reply, "it's the wife's bum. She died a few weeks ago an' ah buried her there, bum up."

"Was this so you would never lose touch with her?"

"Naw! It's so I have somewhere tae park ma bike!"

* * *

The woman said to the greengrocer, "I'll take a pound of these red grapes. My husband just loves them. Do you know if they have been sprayed with any kind of poison?"

"Sorry," replied the grocer. "You'll have to get that at the chemist."

* * *

"You know, Jamima," said her friend, "whenever I'm down in the dumps I just get myself a new hat."

"Mind you, ah wondered where you got them from."

* * *

The chap was at the doctor. "Doctor, I just don't seem to have any energy to do any tasks around the house. I am so tired that all I can do is sit and watch television and occasionally manage to get myself a wee drink."

"Right," said the doctor, "let's examine you."

Ten minutes later the man said, "Okay, just tell me the worst. What is my problem?"

"Well," said the doctor, "if I may be blunt, you're a lazy, drunken bum."

"Okay," said the guy, "but can you give me a medical word for it so I can tell the wife?"

* * *

"Listen tae this, lads," said the man to his mates in the pub. "Last night when ah wis in here a burglar broke into ma hoose."

"Did he get anything?"

"Aye, a broken nose and two teeth knocked oot. The wife thought it wis me coming in drunk!"

* * *

A lady on a train was admiring three tiny babies in the arms of the man opposite her.

"What bonny babies. What are their names?" she asked.

"I dinna ken."

"And just what kind of a man doesn't even know the names of his own weans?"

"I didna say I was the father."

"Then just who are you, and exactly what are you doing with these babies?"

"I'm a salesman for the Scottish Condom Company. They're complaints."

* * *

The woman went to the Registry Office to register her sixth child. The registrar said to her, "Nice to see you again. Congratulations on your latest addition. Now, I assume as usual you wish to call the baby after a famous

film star. So, who is it to be this time, John Wayne, Richard Gere or maybe Brad Pitt?"

"No, this time I thought I would call him Orson, after Orson Welles."

"But Mrs Cart, you can't possibly call him after Orson!"

* * *

The lady at the supermarket checkout was fumbling in her handbag for her purse when a TV remote fell out.

"Do you always carry your TV remote with you or did you accidentally slip it into your bag?" asked the assistant.

"Nothing like that, dear. Ma husband widnae come shopping today, so I reckoned this was the worst thing ah could do tae him."

* * *

The Edinburgh businessman was dying. He called his lawyer to his deathbed and, after ordering his wife not to be upset, started to dispose of his worldly possessions.

"My Rolls Royce I leave to my son, William."

"Better you leave it to James," his wife interrupted. "He's a better driver."

"So let it be James," he whispered. "My Porsche I leave to Ian."

"You had better give it to your nephew, Duncan," his wife again interrupted. "He likes fast cars."

"All right, give it to Duncan. Now my Mercedes 500 I give to my niece, Joanna."

"Personally, I think Fiona should get it."

Unable to take any more, he just managed to raise his head from the pillow and shouted, "Listen, who's dying? You or me?"

* * *

The wee Scottish soldier was startled by a guard as he was trying to sneak out of the camp in England.

"Where's your pass?" demanded the guard.

"Ah dinnae have one. Ah've got a date in town," replied the soldier.

"If you try to leave the barracks I may have to shoot you," said the guard.

The wee Scottish soldier shrugged, walked out the gate and shouted back, "Ah've a mither up in Heaven, a faither doon in hell, and ah've got a hot bit o' stuff in town. And tonight ah'm gonny see wan o' them!"

* * *

"Now children," said the mother. "I have something to tell you about yer Uncle Bob. He's had a sex change at a private hospital in Edinburgh."

"A sex change?"

"Aye. Snip, snip, snip, and Bob's yer auntie!"

* * *

The man knocked at his neighbour's door.

"Listen, Andy, dae ye like women wi big bellies?"

"Naw."

"Dae ye like women wi saggy boobs?"

"Naw."

"Dae ye like women that never clean their hoose?"

"Naw."

"Dae ye like women that dae nothing but nag?"

"Naw."

"Right, then. Keep yer filthy hauns aff ma wife!"

* * *

The Scottish father said to his daughter, "Yer boyfriend asked me for yer hand in marriage and I gave him ma blessing."

"But Dad, I don't want to leave Mum."

"I understand that, dear. Don't let me stand in the way of your happiness. Take yer mother with you!"

* * *

Two men were talking in the Highland village pub. "Ah hate tae tell you this, Fergus, but that lassie o' yours is a right slapper. She's sleeping wi' every man in the village."

"Och, indeed. Tut, tut. Mind you it could well be a great deal worse."

"How could it get worse?" asked his friend.

"Well, we could be living in a town."

* * *

The driver stopped his bus at a stop and on came a lady and her son. She held out her money for the tickets and said, "One and a half, driver."

The driver looked at the boy and said, "Listen, musses, that boy is sixteen if he's a day."

The lady haughtily replied. "I'll have you know, driver, I've only been married fourteen years."

"Listen, hen," said the driver. "Ah'm only takin' fares. No' confessions!"

* * *

Two farmers' wives in Ayrshire were talking.

"See that bull we bought a month ago. Useless! We put him in wi the coos an' he husnae gone near ony o' them."

"Did ye buy him in Mull?"

"As a matter o' fact we did."

"Aye, sadly ma husband's fae there, tae."

* * *

"You are looking smart and confident these days," remarked Eleanor to her friend Lynne.

"Yes," replied Lynne. "I used to have a bit of an inferiority complex but I cured it completely."

"Just how did you manage that?" asked Eleanor.

"I was sick in bed for a day while my husband managed the household and the children!"

* * *

The Scot had won ten million on Lotto. He was interviewed on STV. "What are you going to do with your winnings?" asked the interviewer.

"Well, ah'm going to spend a quarter of it on whisky, beer and lager. Then another quarter on horses, the dogs and fitba. Then another quarter on women and loose living."

"And what will you do with the remaining two and a half million?" asked the interviewer.

"Och, I'll probably jist fritter it away."

* * *

"I hear Wee Sammy ran away from the altar."

"Lost his nerve, I suppose?"

"No, found it."

* * *

The long funeral cortege made its way slowly through the streets of Glasgow. One of the two hearses carried the coffin, the other was overflowing with flowers.

Many people stopped to see this prestigious affair.

"Whose funeral is that?" asked one wee passer-by to a policeman. "It must be somebody awful important."

"Aye," replied a policeman, "it's Big Wullie MacGonigal's girlfriend."

"Big Wullie the gangster's girlfriend? Whit did she die o'?"

"Gonorrhoea."

"Gonorrhoea! Naebuddy dies nooadays wi' gonorrhoea."

"Ye dae if ye give it tae Big Wullie."

TOURISM

"We'll just stop here," said the wife. "It's an ideal spot for a picnic."

"It must be," replied her husband. "Fifty million midges cannae be wrong."

* * *

High above Glencoe a lonely eagle soared looking for companionship. Suddenly it saw a frog in amongst the heather. The eagle swooped and had his wicked way with the frog. At the end of which the frog turned to the eagle and said, "Ah'm a wee frog, and we've had a wee snog, goodbye!"

The following day the eagle again felt lonely as it floated on the thermals above the Glen. Then it saw a hare running through the rocks. The eagle swooped and had his wicked way with the hare. At the end of which the hare turned to the eagle and said, "Ah'm a wee hare, and we've had an affair. Goodbye!"

The next day the eagle was again lonely. This time it saw a duck in a loch. The eagle swooped and had his wicked way with the duck. At the end of which the duck turned to the eagle and said, "You've made a mistake. Ah'm a wee drake!"

* * *

A huge, muscled tourist goes into a Glasgow pub. He is just about to start his tenth pint of beer when he feels the call of nature. Knowing that Glasgow is a tough town he puts a note under his pint glass. 'This pint belongs to the Heavyweight Boxing Champion of the World.'

On his return he finds the glass empty and another note. 'This pint is inside the One Hundred Yards Sprint Champion of Glasgow.'

* * *

In a Highland village hall the audience listened to an English touring orchestra playing Haydn's Farewell Symphony. In this piece one player after another quietly lays down their musical instrument and tiptoes offstage. Two old Scots in the audience looked on in astonishment as the last musician disappeared, leaving only the conductor on the stage.

One turned to the other and observed, "See, they Sassanachs just cannae haud their whisky, Hamish."

* * *

The tourist phoned the hotel's night porter at three o'clock in the morning.

"This is room 345. Ah gotta leak in the sink."

"Aye, OK. Go ahead."

* * *

The leading lady at one of the Edinburgh Festival productions was in a dreadful mood.

"What's the matter with her?" asked the stage director.

"She only got two bouquets presented to her tonight at the end of the show."

"So? Isn't that enough for her?"

"No. She ordered three."

* * *

Two tourists wandered into a pub in Glasgow. "Nice to see an old fashioned bar with sawdust on the floor, barman," drawled one of the tourists.

"Don't be daft, sur. That's last night's furniture."

* * *

The American tourist had been fishing on a Scottish river for two weeks. On his last day he finally caught a salmon. Turning to the gillie he observed, "You know, this salmon has cost me over ten thousand dollars."

"Well, sur," replied the gillie. "Are ye no' lucky ye didnae catch more than one."

* * *

The Scot stood admiring the might of Niagara Falls. An American nearby said, "No Scotsman could create anything like that. Huh?"

"Yer right, Yank. But ah know a Polish plumber who could fix it!"

* * *

An American was being shown around Edinburgh by his Scottish relative. They came to Holyrood Palace.

"How long did it take to build this palace?" asked the American.

"I believe it took more than twenty years," replied his relative.

"You Scots must be lazy. In America this would have been built in ten years."

They then went over to the Scottish Parliament

Building. "And how long did it take to build this Parliament?" asked the American.

"Five years."

"You Scots must be lazy. In America this would have been built in two years."

Finally they came to Edinburgh Castle. "And how long did it take to build this castle?" asked the American.

"I don't know. It wisnae there yesterday!"

* * *

One dark, stormy night in the Highlands, a tourist got lost. The rain was torrential and as he made his way along a roadside, he could hardly see more than a few feet in front of him.

Suddenly he became conscious of a car coming up behind him, then it stopped. Desperate for shelter he opened the passenger door and got in the car. The ghostlike car started to move, and the tourist became aware that there was no driver, and the engine wasn't switched on.

The tourist looked ahead and saw a sharp bend approaching. Scared, he prayed for his life. In answer to his prayer a hand appeared through the driver's window and, just in the nick of time, turned the wheel.

The lights of a roadside inn appeared and the tourist gathered his strength, opened the door, threw himself out and ran screaming into the inn.

Wet and shaking, he knocked back two double whiskies in quick succession. Then he quickly told everyone in the bar about his terrifying experience.

Ten minutes later, two kilted Highlanders entered the bar. Both were soaked and breathing hard. Seeing the tourist, one turned to the other and said, "Look Hamish. There's that bleedin' idiot who got in the car while we were pushing it!"

* * *

The English tourist was a first class golfer, playing off a very low handicap. At a golf course in a small Highland town he was just about to start playing when he saw an old golfer shuffling out from the golf club.

"Do you fancy a round?" asked the young man.

"Certainly, young sur," came the reply. "And tae make it interesting we should play for a penny a hole and ten pounds for the last hole."

"Fair enough," replied the tourist, and off they went.

The tourist easily won the first seventeen holes. At the last hole the choice was either to hit the ball the long way round a dog-leg, or hit the ball over a huge pine tree beyond which lay the green.

"Aye," said the Highlander. "When ah wis your age ah hit the ball right o'er that tree."

"Right," said the tourist. Gritting his teeth he gave the ball an almighty smack. It almost made the top of the tree but hit the top branches before bouncing and landing back on the tee.

"Mind you," said the Highlander. "When ah wis your age yon pine tree wis six feet high!"

* * *

"Did you hear about the tourist in the Highlands who tried to beat a speeding train to a level crossing?"

"No. Did he get across?"

"Aye. A marble one with his name on it."

* * *

The tourist was absolutely blootered. He had been at the whisky all day. He stumbled out of the Hilton in Glasgow, fell into a taxi, and said to the cabbie, "Take me to the Hilton, driver."

"We're there, sir," said the driver.

"Ok," said the tourist giving the driver a tenner. "Keep the change. But see next time, don't drive so fast!"

* * *

A very shy Englishman visited an island in the Western Isles where the inhabitants only spoke Gaelic. He stayed at the home of a local fisherman who was keen to learn the English terms for various words.

One day the Englishman and the fisherman were tramping through the heather when they came upon a shepherd urinating. The fisherman looked at the bashful Englishman and raised an enquiring brow. "Ah . . . em," stuttered the Sassanach, "er . . . it's . . . irrigating the ground."

They then came across a crofter defecating behind a stone dyke. The fisherman pointed to the man, clearly wanting to know the English term. "Em . . . it's eh . . . fertilizing the land," he said.

Soon they came across a small wood and saw a couple copulating. The fisherman again indicated he wished to know the name of this activity.

"Oh . . . em . . . that's . . . em . . . riding a bicycle," stuttered the Englishman.

The following day the fisherman took the Englishman out on his boat. As they sailed past a lonely beach the fisherman suddenly went red in the face, and pointed at a couple copulating on the sand.

"Oh . . . em . . . that's . . . em . . . riding a bicycle again," said the Englishman.

"But sur," said the fisherman struggling to talk English. "He riding ma bicycle!"

* * *

"Aye, I have a wonderful Scottish family heritage," the Scot was telling the North American tourist. "In fact one of my ancestors was killed at the Battle of Culloden in 1746."

"Wow! Was he in Bonnie Prince Charlie's army?"

"No. No. He was actually camping nearby and went over to complain about the noise!"

* * *

The taxi driver picked up a Japanese passenger at Edinburgh Airport. "St Andrews," said the tourist.

Just as they left the airport a car zoomed past.

"Honda, very fast. Made in Japan," observed the tourist.

Going over the Forth Road Bridge another car flew past.

"Toyota, very fast. Made in Japan," observed the tourist.

Half an hour on another car flew past.

"Mitsubishi, very fast. Made in Japan."

Finally the taxi arrived in St Andrews. The fare was five hundred pounds. The Japanese said, "My goodness, very expensive."

"Aye," said the fed up driver. "Meter, very fast. Made in Japan."

* * *

An American tourist has a terrible accident in Edinburgh. The city tour bus he is getting off runs over his feet and he loses three of his toes.

In Edinburgh Infirmary, with his foot swathed in bandages, he is visited by the director of VisitScotland. "We were so sorry to hear of your dreadful accident. However I have done something to cheer you up. Your wife tells me your favourite singer is Al Jolson, and I have arranged for the hospital radio to play one of his songs at five o'clock tonight."

The chap switched the hospital radio on at 5pm and listened to Al Jolson singing 'Toot, toot, tootsie goodbye!'.

* * *

On a train between Glasgow and Edinburgh, an American tourist addressed himself to the old Scotsman sitting opposite him patiently reading his paper.

"Say, Scotty, you Scots are only proud of one thing; being Scottish. Look at me. I may be American but I have French blood, Italian blood, German blood with a little Greek thrown in. What do you think o' that, Scotty?"

The Scot looked up and slowly replied. "What do ah think o' that? Ah think it wis very sporting o' yer mother."

* * *

A tourist in Aberdeen was proving to be a little irritating in a restaurant. First of all he complained that it was too hot and demanded that the head waiter turn the air conditioning on. Then, not long afterwards, he complained that it was too cold and the air conditioning be turned down. All night he was either too hot or too cold, continually making demands of the poor head waiter.

At the end of the evening another guest, while settling his bill, said to the head waiter, "By jove, I must compliment you on the remarkable resilience you showed with that fellow and his demands about the air conditioning."

"Didnae bother me, sur. We huvnae got any air conditioning."

* * *

A man took his next-door neighbour to Glasgow airport, where he was to meet his sister who had emigrated to New Zealand some forty years ago.

"Will she recognise you?" asked the man.

"Och, aye. Sure ah havenae been away."

* * *

An American tourist books into a bed and breakfast in Scotland. The following morning he finds himself desperate for a dump, and as there is no en-suite he has a problem. He manages to make the bathroom at the end of the corridor but it is occupied. He is now in a desperate state.

So back in his bedroom he does the business on a newspaper on the floor. Then he has the problem of disposing of it. He sees a large plant pot in the corner, lifts out the plant and puts the poo underneath.

A week later he is back in the States when he receives an email: 'Dear Ex-Guest. All is forgiven. We know what you did. Please, please, please just tell us where you hid it.'

* * *

The Glasgow Scots-Italian stud picked up a gorgeous blonde tourist and soon they were in bed having energetic sex.

Finally they stopped, he lit a cigarette, raised his eyebrows and mumbled, "You finish?"

She smiled provocatively and replied, "No."

"Well, nae burda mine leavesa unsatisfied." And there followed an hour of love making.

He wearily got out of bed, raised his eyebrows and mumbled, "You finish noo, eh?"

She again smiled provocatively and replied, "No."

After another hour, and shattered by his exertions, he croaked hopefully. "You finish noo?"

"No finish."

"How you no' finish?"

"Me Swedish!"

* * *

The American tourist was going around a Scottish town. He got chatting to a local. "Say, any really big men ever born in this town?"

"Naw, jist wee weans."

* * *

An old Scottish lady from the Western Isles goes to her local travel agent and books a flight to Calcutta. The travel agent tries to persuade her against this as he believes that Calcutta is not the sort of place for an old lady tourist. However she persists and sets off for Calcutta.

After a long journey she arrives in Calcutta, and gets into a rickety old bus going into the hot and dusty interior of India. After three days the bus finally gets to a town. There she joins a queue outside a temple waiting to see a famous guru.

One of the temple priests, seeing that the old lady is clearly exhausted, tries to persuade her that she should rest at a nearby hotel, but no, she insists on waiting in the hot sun to see the guru. After six hours the old lady finally gets to the head of the queue. A priest whispers that she is only allowed to say twelve words to the famous guru.

The moment arrives and the old lady finds herself standing in front of an old man dressed in a loin-cloth, sitting cross legged on a small platform. A priest tells her that she can now say her dozen words.

"Right, Jimmy MacGregor. Get yer claes oan. Yer comin' hame right noo!"

* * *

A tourist and his wife went to a show at the Fringe at the Edinburgh Festival. He became desperate for a pee, and during the interval hurried off to find a toilet.

He couldn't find any toilets but he did come across an ornamental vase. He decided to do it there and then.

When he got back to his seat the second act had already started. "Did I miss much?" he whispered to his wife.

"Miss it?" she said. "You were in it!"

* * *

The Texan was visiting Scotland, and every time his host showed him a sight he would say, "That's nothing! We've got the same thing back in Texas, only better!"

Finally they came to Loch Lomond. The Texan said, "Well, finally we have found one thing we don't have in Texas. This is indeed a pretty loch."

His host replied, "Well, you could run a pipeline from Texas under the Atlantic to the loch. If you can suck as hard as you can blow, the loch is all yours."

* * *

The English tourist was talking to a Clan Chief in the Highlands. "England has brought civilization to many continents. In your opinion how have we English improved Scotland?"

"Well, before you English ventured north of the border, there were no taxes, no debts, plenty fish, plenty deer and plenty whisky. The Scot spent his day hunting, fishing and distilling whisky. The Scot spent his nights having sex. Only the English would be dumb enough to assume they could improve on a system like that!"

* * *

An American billionaire was travelling in Scotland when he stopped at Scotty's Café for a cup of coffee. He was astonished at the bill. "Fifty pounds for a cup of coffee?" he asked. "Is coffee so rare in Scotland?"

"No," replied Scotty. "But American billionaires are!"

* * *

The tourist and his wife went to an Italian fish and chip restaurant in Edinburgh. They ordered fish and chips, and just as they were about to start eating the woman noticed that there was no salt on the table. Her husband called over the Italian waiter, and explained there was no salt. The Italian put his hand in his right hand trouser pocket, brought out a pinch of salt, and scattered it on top of their fish suppers.

Again, as they were just about to start eating the man noticed there was no pepper. He called the waiter over and told him there appeared to be no pepper available. The waiter reached into the left hand pocket of his trousers, produced pepper, and duly sprinkled it on their fish suppers.

Just as the couple were going to start eating, the wife whispered to the husband. "For heaven's sake don't ask for vinegar!"

* * *

In Aberdeen a man took his overseas guests to a steak restaurant. "I was in this restaurant last week and I had the biggest, most delicious, steak I ever had in my life," he told them.

The group sat at a nice table at the back of the restaurant, and all ordered steak.

When the steaks came they were the smallest steaks any of them had ever seen.

"See here," protested the embarrassed Scot to the waitress.

"Last week I was here and you served me with a massive, juicy steak. What is the meaning of this?"

"Well," said the waitress. "Last week ye were sittin' at yon table next to the window."

OLD SCOTTIES

The elderly lady pulled into the supermarket car park. She then half rolled down a rear window to make sure her retriever had sufficient fresh air. Carefully getting out of the car she moved a few yards away before instructing, "Now you stay. Be good. Stay! Stay!"

An old fellow passing by gave her a strange look and observed, "Hey musses. Why don't ye just pit oan yer handbrake."

* * *

Miss McDuff was the church organist, had never married, and was in her late eighties. One day the minister came to see her at her home.

Sitting in her lounge while she prepared tea, he noticed that there was a small Hammond organ in the room. On the top of the musical instrument was a bowl filled with water, and on top of the water floated a condom.

As they sat talking, his eyes continually drifted to the bowl and eventually he could no longer contain his curiosity. "I was wondering, Miss McDuff," he began, "if you could tell me about . . . er . . . your bowl."

"Oh, yes," said Miss McDuff, "Isn't it just grand. I was walking through the park over a year ago and I found this little package on the ground. The directions said that it should be placed on the organ, kept wet, and it would prevent the spread of disease. And do you know I haven't had a cold all winter."

* * *

The old Scot had emigrated to Canada many years previously. Tonight was Hogmanay and he had got fu'. He lay by the roadside peacefully sleeping.

In the morning a man passed by with a live chicken under his arm. The bird was squawking and its wings were flapping.

The man carrying the chicken noticed that the old Scot had wakened, and more than that, was crying.

"Are you alright?" he asked.

"Aye, I'm fine," replied the Scot. "It's just that when I hear the pipes it aye brings a tear tae ma eye."

* * *

There was a raffle down at the Old Folk's Club and life long friends, Jimmy, Rory and Finlay all bought a ticket. Amazingly they all won prizes. Jimmy won a bottle of wine, Rory won a box of chocolates and Finlay a toilet brush.

The following week they were discussing their success in the raffle. Jimmy said that he and his wife had enjoyed the wine, Rory and his wife had loved the chocolates, but bachelor Finlay complained that the toilet brush was no good. He was going back to paper.

* * *

One Sunday Jenny heard that her grandfather had died and immediately went to visit her granny in their house on a Glasgow housing estate.

"And how and when did poor Grandpa die?"

"Well, it is a wee bit embarrassing, dear, but this morning we were making love and sadly, he had a heart attack."

"Granny, you're both nearly ninety, surely that kind of activity was just asking for trouble?"

"Well, it has been our habit for many years now to have sex on a Sunday morning, you know, slowly, in time with the church bells. Ding, dong, ding dong."

"So, what went wrong?"

"Well, a blooming ice-cream van stopped outside . . ."

* * *

The Scotsman of eighty-five married a young lady of eighteen, and a year after the wedding his wife had a baby. The husband went to visit his wife and the child at the local maternity unit. "My," said the sister in charge, "you really are a fit man for your age."

"Aye, sister," he replied, "you've got to keep the engine running."

A year on, another baby arrived, and again the husband visited the maternity unit.

"My," said the same sister in charge. "You really, really are a fit man for your age."

"Aye, sister," he replied, "you've got to keep the engine running."

A further year on, yet another baby arrived. Again the husband visited the maternity unit.

"Nice to see you again," said the sister.

"Aye, sister," he replied, "you've got to keep the engine running."

"Well, ye better change yer oil," she replied. "This wan's black!"

* * *

The tiny old man shuffled slowly into the café, stood to get back his breath before painfully sitting down. The waitress came over and he ordered a banana split.

The waitress smiled and asked, "Crushed nuts?"

"Naw hen, arthritis."

* * *

Two old Scots were talking. "You know, Jock, ah just love the way you address your dear wife. You never call her by her name but just use all these wonderful terms of endearment. Ma wee pet, ma sweet wee wifie, darling, precious lamb, ma wee honey. It really shows your love for her."

"Love for her? Listen, the truth is ah forgot her name years ago!"

* * *

An older woman, whose husband had gone missing, went to the police station with a friend. "My dear husband is missing. He's about forty, six feet three, bright blue eyes, dark wavy hair, keeps himself in shape, weighs twelve and a half stones, good teeth, is kind, has a great sense of humour, and is good with animals and children."

"Hold on," her friend protested. "Your husband is sixty-five, five feet two, is half-blind, has no hair left, is at least fifteen stones, has false teeth, is a miserable sod and hates animals and children."

"Ah know. But who wid want him back?"

* * *

At the plane crash site, the lone survivor, an old Scot, sat with his back to a tree, chewing a bone. As he tossed the bone onto a huge pile of bones he noticed the rescue team. "Thank heavens," he cried out in relief.

The rescue team came to a sudden halt. They were in shock at the sight of the pile of human bones.

The survivor saw the horror on their faces and said, "You

cannae judge me on this. I had tae survive. We Scots are a tough bunch. Throughout our history we've had to struggle to succeed. Is it so wrong wantin' tae live?"

The leader of the rescue party spoke. "I cannot judge you for wanting to survive . . . but your plane only crashed yesterday."

* * *

Two elderly widows in Edinburgh were talking.

"Mabel, that nice widower John Mackintosh has asked me to go out on a date with him. I know you went out on a date with him recently and I wanted to talk to you before I gave him an answer."

"Well, Christine, let me tell you what happened. He showed up at my flat at seven o'clock prompt, brought me flowers, and off we went in his new Jaguar to the best restaurant in town. It was a beautiful meal, champagne, the lot. It was just lovely and he was so charming. Then, when he took me home he turned into a wild beast. He went completely crazy. Tore off my expensive new dress and had his wicked way with me . . . twice."

"Goodness gracious. So, are you telling me I shouldn't go out with him?"

"No, no. All I'm saying is . . . wear an old dress."

* * *

Sammy decided to introduce his granny to the internet. He sat the old lady down in front of his PC. He showed her how to log on then said that they should try his search engine. "Ah'm a wee bitty nervous on this internet thingmy," she exclaimed.

"Listen, Gran," he said. "All you've got to do is type in a question. Just pretend you're asking someone a question."

"Aw right, Sammy," she said. "Ah'll gie it a go."

She then typed in: 'How is ma sister in Pitlochry keeping?'

* * *

Two elderly ladies were discussing their husbands. "I do wish ma John would stop biting his nails. It just grates on ma nerves."

"Ma Jock used to do that but I cured him of the habit."

"So, tell me," asked the first lady. "What did you do?"

"Ah hid his teeth."

* * *

The two sweet, old Scottish ladies were chatting. The conversation stopped and one shyly said, "Listen, the truth is that I know you and me have been friends for many years. But I'm very, very sorry, I cannot remember your name."

She then looked on as her friend's face showed great sadness as she struggled to cope with this news.

Eventually she replied, "How soon do you need to know?"

* * *

A 78 year-old grandmother was arrested in Glasgow for prostitution. Not only did she have sex with clients, on their birthday she also sent them a card with five pounds.

* * *

Two old chaps in a care home were talking.

"Ah've got tae tell you that since ah came intae this place ah'm getting a little action."

"Dae ye mean sex?"

"Naw, naw. Ah'm referring tae the prune juice!"

* * *

"Whit are you doing sitting in that chair looking as white as a sheet, Willie," said the old lady to her husband one morning.

"Well, ye see, Maggie. Ah pit oan ma shirt and a button fell aff, then ah opened the bedroom door and the handle fell aff, and . . . you know how these things tend tae go in threes?"

"Aye, but whit's the problem?"

"Ah need tae wee!"

* * *

Willie was at the funeral of Tam's dad, a rich old Highlander who had died at the age of a hundred and ten.

"Sorry to hear your dad died, Tam. Somebody told me it wis cancer."

"Naw, naw. He had cancer in his sixties and recovered," replied Tam.

"Somebody else told me he had a heart attack," said Willie.

"Naw, naw. He had a heart attack in his seventies, got a by-pass and recovered."

"Somebody else said it was the drink."

"Naw, naw. He had a problem wi the drink in his eighties but he gave it up and recovered."

"Somebody else told me he was knocked down by a car."

"Naw, naw. He was knocked down by a car in his nineties but he recovered."

"Well, somebody else told me he had drowned."

"Naw, naw. He started swimming in the loch when he was a hundred and five, nearly drowned one day but recovered."

"He sounded indestructible," commented Willie.

"You're right. That's whit ah thought tae. In the end ah had tae shoot the bugger!"

* * *

"You'll never guess what happened to me last night," said Janet, a spinster, to her married friend Rose. "An old man stopped me in the street and showed me the lining of his coat."

"Are you sure he only wanted you to see the lining of his coat?"

"Oh, aye. He wasn't wearing anything else."

* * *

The old Scottish soldier was celebrating his 99th birthday.

He spoke to his toes. "How are you toes? You were soaked in the trenches in 1916 but you are 99 years old today."

He spoke to his knees. "How are you knees? You marched proudly in the victory parade but you are 99 years old today."

He spoke to his crotch. "Hello Willy. If you were alive today you would have been 99 years old."

* * *

The attractive young lady with two heavy shopping bags got on a bus in Princes Street in Edinburgh. The bus was absolutely full but she managed to stand on the lower deck. On a seat was an old gentleman who courteously doffed his hat and said, "I'm sorry for not giving you my seat, my dear, but I am getting on a bit. But if you like I will put your shopping bags on my knee."

"That's very kind of you," she said. "But I have been on my feet for hours and perhaps I might sit on your lap."

So, the young lady sat on the old gentleman's lap as the bus rumbled on its way. About ten minutes later the old gentleman spoke to her. "I am sorry, my dear, but I must ask you to stand up. Apparently I am not as old as I thought I was!"

* * *

An old Scot went into a chemist shop and asked for a packet of Viagra, then asked the chemist if he would kindly cut the tablets into quarters.

"But, sir," protested the chemist. "At your age a quarter of a tablet won't give you a full erection."

"That's ok," said the old fella. "Ah don't want a full erection. Ah jist want it to stick oot far enough so ah don't pee on ma new shoes."

* * *

In the fabric department of a large store, a pretty girl asked the male assistant, "How much does this dress material cost?"

"For you," he said with a smirk, "one kiss per yard."

"That's fine," she replied. "I'll take four yards."

The assistant duly measured out the material and wrapped it for the girl. Then he closed his eyes and pursed his lips.

The girl picked up the package, turned to the elderly man nearby, and said, "Right Grandpa, pay the man!"

* * *

A ninety-year-old Scot married a ninety-year-old woman. On their wedding night they both got into bed, the old fellow held her hand and they drifted off to sleep.

The following evening the pair got into bed, the old fellow held her hand and they drifted off to sleep.

The next night the pair got into bed, and the old man reached out to hold her hand but she pulled it away. "Not tonight, dear," she said. "I'm too tired."

* * *

An elderly lady was flying from Glasgow to London to see her sister. She had never flown before and, as it was

a low-budget airline, seats were not allocated. However, she did manage to find a comfortable seat.

Soon a man came along and insisted he wanted her seat, but as it was a nice seat with a great view she would not move.

"Okay," said the man. "In that case, madam, you fly the bloomin' plane!"

* * *

It was 1746, just after the Battle of Culloden. Cumberland's troops arrived in a wee Scottish hamlet. "Bring us food," demanded the Officer.

"All we have left is half a loaf."

"War is war," said the officer, and took the bread.

"Now, bring us whisky," he demanded.

"All we have left is half a bottle of whisky."

"War is war," said the officer, and took the bottle.

"Bring us a woman," demanded the officer.

"But there is only one left in the village."

"War is war," said the officer.

Out came an eighty-eight-year-old granny. The officer took one look at her and said, "Okay, we'll let you off this time."

"Not on your nellie," said granny. "War is war!"

* * *

A ninety-four year old man in Inverness married an eighteen-year-old girl.

Her friends gave her crystal glasses . . . and his friends gave him six weeks!

* * *

A young chap in Edinburgh was in Tesco when he became aware that an old lady was following him. In fact at the checkout queue she was just in front of him. She turned and said, "Sorry if I seemed to be following you, but you fair look like ma son who died last year."

"Sorry to hear that," replied the young man, "is there anything I can do for you?"

"Yes," she said sadly, "as I'm leaving can you shout 'Cheerio, Mum!' That would really cheer me up."

"Of course," he replied.

As the old woman was leaving he duly called out, "Cheerio, Mum!", and she gave him a kindly smile and wave.

When he came to pay for his groceries the bill came to over a hundred pounds. "You must have made a mistake," he said to the assistant. "I only bought a few things."

"That's true," replied the assistant, "but your mother said you were paying for her stuff."

* * *

Two old guys were talking. "For our 50th wedding anniversary I'm taking my wife to New Zealand."

"Wow. That's some distance. That will be a hard act to follow. So what are you going to do on your 60th anniversary?"

"I'm going to go back and get her!"

* * *

The old Scot was a few months off his hundredth birthday. He sent a letter to the Queen saying that he would celebrate his hundredth birthday by making love to his ninety-eight-year-old wife.

When he reached a hundred the Queen sent him a telegram and the Duke of Edinburgh sent him a diagram.

* * *

Three elderly Scots, one from Perth, one from Edinburgh and one from Glasgow, were standing

together urinating in a public toilet at a football ground.

The Glaswegian, in the middle, looked down to his right and noticed that the chap from Perth was producing two streams. "What's the matter wi' you, pal?"

"Took a bullet in the war. They had to remove my privates and now I've just got two holes."

The Glaswegian looked to his left and the chap from Edinburgh was producing three streams. "And what's the matter wi you, pal?"

"War wound as well. Shrapnel got me, and now I've got no privates, just three holes."

The guys from Perth and Edinburgh now looked at the Glaswegian in the middle and together said, "And whit's the matter with you, old chap. Looks like you've got twenty streams. Old war wound?"

"Naw, ma zip's stuck."

* * *

Two old Scots meet in the street. One of them had lost an arm in the war.

"Where are you going, Andrew?" asked one.

"Ah'm going to change a light-bulb," replied the chap with one arm.

"Won't that be a bit difficult with the one arm?"

"Naw, naw. I've got the receipt."

* * *

The old lady's car was stopped by the police on the A9.

"Excuse me madam, but you were weaving all over the road."

"Thank goodness you're here, officer. I just got new

bi-focals in Perth and every time I look up I now see a tree coming towards me. So I swerve and there is another tree right in front of me. It's terrifying!"

"Madam, there is no tree. It's your air freshener!"

* * *

Due to the price of modern hearing aids, a Scotsman wrapped a piece of wire around his ear and tucked the other end into his top jacket pocket. "Do you hear better now with that wire around yer ear?" asked a friend.

"Naw, ah canne hear ony better," came the reply, "but everybody certainly talks louder."

* * *

Two old men were talking. "Listen, Ian. Ah'm that pleased. Ah managed to make love tae ma wife last night fur three minutes."

"Och, that's nothing, Andy. Last March ah made love tae ma wife fur an hour and three minutes."

"Wow, you must be fit."

"Naw, it wis the night they pit the clocks forward."

* * *

Grandpa announced to his family that he was going to marry again. "I've been a widower too long," he said. "So I've asked that wee lassie o' nineteen doon the road tae marry me."

"But," protested his daughter. "Imagine a man of eighty-six marrying a girl of only nineteen."

"Whit's wrang wi that?" inquired the old man. "That's exactly the same age your mother was when ah married her!"

* * *

The old man settled himself into the barber's chair. "Before you start," he said to the barber, "ah know the weather's terrible, ah don't care who wins the Old Firm match on Saturday, ah canny afford holidays, ah don't bet on the gee-gees, ah know ah'm gettin' thin on top, ah'm getting a wee bit deaf, so, just get on with it."

"Ok, pal," said the barber, "but ah'd be able tae concentrate better if ye didnae talk so much!"

* * *

Fact: Inside every old Scot there's a young Scot wondering what the hell happened!

HEALTH

A world-renowned dietician was addressing a prestigious audience in Edinburgh. "I know that you in Scotland have a most unhealthy diet. In fact the food you put into your mouths is enough to have killed most of you sitting here, years ago.

"Processed meat is dangerous. All soft drinks erode your stomach lining. Chinese food contains MSG. Fried food causes many problems. But there is one food that is the most dangerous of all. And we all have eaten it, or will at some time eat it. Can anyone tell me what this food is that causes so much grief and suffering in the years after it is eaten?"

An elderly man in the back row shouted out. "Wedding cake!"

* * *

The lovely young lady was wheeled by a porter towards the operating theatre. She was wearing nothing and merely covered in a white sheet. The porter left her in the corridor outside the theatre.

A distinguished man wearing a white coat approached, lifted the sheet and stared at her naked body. A second man in a white coat appeared, lifted the sheet and also looked at her naked body. Shortly after, a third man, similarly attired, was just about to lift the sheet when she asked, somewhat irritably, "I appreciate all the attention and examinations, but when am I going to get my operation?"

The man shrugged his shoulders and said, "Sorry, hen, ah know nothin' aboot that. We're just painting this corridor."

* * *

The ninety-year-old man entered his local medical centre.

"Can I help you, sir?" asked the receptionist.

"Ah need tae see a doctor. Ah've a problem wi' ma willy."

"Sir! You cannot possibly just walk in here and say that! Look around you. The waiting area is full of people. It's embarrassing. You should have used another word, like ear. Then when you saw the doctor, told him the real problem privately."

So the old man shuffled out the door, turned around, and came back into the Health Centre.

"Can I help you, sir?" asked the same receptionist.

"Ah need tae see the doctor. Ah cannae piss oot ma ear."

* * *

Two beggars on Princes Street were talking. "Ye know, when ah wis six ah wanted tae become a brain surgeon."

"So, whit scuppered you?"

"They widnae let weans into the operating theatres."

* * *

A patient was seen fleeing down the corridor of a Scottish NHS hospital just before his operation.

A porter stopped him and asked, "What's the matter?"

"Well, I heard a nurse say, 'It's really a very simple operation. Don't worry, it will probably be fine.'"

"She was just trying to comfort you," replied the porter. "Why are you so frightened?"

"She wasn't talking to me. She was talking to the surgeon!"

* * *

Jimmy went to see his doctor and produced a note saying: 'I cannot make any sounds. Can you help?'

The doctor instructed him to take off his shoes and socks. Then he gave an almighty jump and landed on Jimmy's toes.

Jimmy cried in agony, "AAAAAAAAAAAAAAA!"

"Right," said the doctor. "Make another appointment at reception. Next time we'll learn B."

* * *

Two wee boys were in a department store in Edinburgh. They were closely examining bathroom scales.

"What's it for?" one asked.

"You stand on it and it makes you mad!"

* * *

Two men were talking in a pub. "I was reading today that there are five million people in Scotland, three million TV sets and two million bathrooms."

"So whit does that prove?" asked his friend.

"There are a lot o' dirty folk in Scotland watching the telly!"

* * *

Jamie met his friend Keith in the street.

"How's it going?" asked Jamie.

"Terrible," replied Keith. "Last year my house

burned down and I had no insurance. Then the family retriever was killed by a van. Then I checked the lottery numbers I use, they had come up, but I'd forgotten to buy a ticket. Now the doctor has told me I only have three months to live."

"I am so sorry," replied Jamie. "How awful for you."

"Actually it's not all bad," said Keith. "At least the shop is doing well."

"What kind of shop is it?" asked Jamie.

"We sell lucky white heather."

* * *

Two ladies were talking in the street.

"Did ye hear that Agnes has caught a fatal disease. Apparently it hasn't been around since before the First World War."

"For goodness sake. How did she catch it?"

"She got it aff a magazine in her doctor's waiting room."

* * *

A man went to see his doctor about the results of some tests. "I am very sorry," said the doctor, "but you have only a year to live."

"Is there nothing I can do, doctor?" asked the anxious patient.

"Well, you could move to Stenhousemuir, marry the ugliest woman in town, and support the local team."

"And will that cure me?"

"No, but it will make it seem like a long time."

* * *

The wee Glasgow woman and a baby went to the doctor's surgery. The doctor examined the baby and pronounced its weight below average.

"Is the baby breast fed or bottle fed?" he asked.

"Breast fed, doctor."

"Right, strip to the waist, please," he instructed. He then pressed, rolled and pinched both breasts in a rigorous examination.

"No wonder the baby is underweight. You don't have any milk," he said.

"Ah know, doctor. A'm the granny, but ah'm glad ah came."

* * *

The phone rang and the Glasgow housewife answered. "Listen, this is the lab at Glasgow Royal. There's been a wee bit of a mix up with your husband's tests. Either he has Alzheimer's or Aids."

"So what should I do?" asked the anxious wife.

"Take him to Queen Street station and put him on a train for Edinburgh. If he ever comes back, don't sleep with him."

* * *

The nurse had just delivered triplets. She brought them out of the delivery room to show to the father. He could hardly believe his good fortune. As he went to touch them the nurse said, "You can't touch them! You're not sterile!"

The man replied proudly. "You're dead right ah'm no'!"

* * *

"Doctor, every morning when I'm shaving and I look in the mirror, I feel like throwing up. Could you tell me what is wrong with me?"

"I don't know, but at least your eyesight is okay."

* * *

"Doctor, quick," said the receptionist. "can ye deal wi an emergency?"

"Sorry, I can't."

"Please yersel'. But yer wife jist phoned tae say yer hoose is on fire."

* * *

The Dundee wifie went to see her doctor, complaining of stomach pains. After examining her, the doctor told her it was just wind.

"Jist wind!" she exclaimed. "It wis 'jist wind' that blew doon the Tay Bridge!"

* * *

The old man shuffled into the Health Centre. He was almost bent double with arthritis and staggered from side to side holding onto his walking stick. Eventually he managed somehow to sit down, and wait for his name to be called to see the doctor.

When the time came he grasped his stick, struggled to get to his feet and shuffled into the doctor's consulting room.

Ten minutes later he strode out, straight as a ramrod.

"Amazing," exclaimed one of the waiting patients. "What kind of miracle cure did he give you?"

"A longer stick."

* * *

The old Scot went into the hospital outpatients department to see the urologist. At the reception desk he gave his name and date of birth.

"Oh, yes," said the somewhat overbearing receptionist in a very loud, clear voice. "You are here to see the doctor about your impotence. Is that right?"

The old Scot glanced at all the patients in the waiting room who had all by now stopped reading their magazines and were looking at him.

In an equally loud tone he replied, "Nae, naw, hen. Ah've come tae enquire aboot a sex change operation, and ah'd like the same surgeon that did yours."

* * *

A wee boy was taken to the hospital to see his new baby twin sisters. After a while the novelty of the twins wore off, and he wandered into another ward. There he started talking to a woman who was covered in bandages.

"How long have you been here?" he asked.

"Nearly two months, son."

"Can ah see yer wee baby?"

"I haven't got a baby, son."

"For goodness sake. You're awfa slow. Ma mither has been in here only a day and she's got two."

* * *

The receptionist buzzed through to the doctor. "Doctor, ye had better take wan o' yer ain tranquilisers gey quick."

"How's that?" asked the doctor.

"39–25–38 is here wantin' another examination again!"

* * *

The unpopular medical student approached the patient in the hospital bed. In his hand he held a syringe. "Nothing to worry about," he said. "Just a little prick with a needle."

"Ah can see that," replied the patient. "But what are you going to do?"

* * *

Every chair in the Health Centre was filled. Over twenty people were standing. The buzz of conversation

died down at one point. During the silence an old fellow wearily stood up and remarked, "Well, ah guess I'll just awa hame and die a death frae natural causes."

* * *

A man with a winking problem applied for a sales job with a large company.

The interviewer told him, "Your qualifications and experience are ideal. However a sales rep must have ideal social skills and your constant winking would embarrass and scare off potential customers."

"Hold on," said the applicant. "If I just take two aspirin I stop winking."

"Really. Can you demonstrate this?"

The applicant reached into his pockets. In every one he pulled out packet after packet of condoms. Eventually he found his aspirins, and after taking two stopped winking.

"Very interesting," said the interviewer. "However this is a respectable company and we do not employ womanisers."

"I'm not a womaniser. I'm a happily married man."

"So explain all these condoms, please."

"Well, have you ever walked into a chemist shop, winking, and asked for aspirin?"

* * *

The bricklayer went to his doctor complaining of constipation.

"Right, strip from the waist down and bend over my desk," ordered the doctor. He then got a golf club and gave the bricklayer's bottom an almighty blow.

"Now go to the toilet down the hall and see how you get on."

Five minutes later the chap was back. "Wonderful, doc. I had a great movement."

"Good," said the doctor. "Just don't wipe your bum with empty cement bags in future."

* * *

The old Scot was on the operating table awaiting a heart operation. Before being anaesthetized he insisted on talking to his son, a well-respected surgeon, who was carrying out the operation.

"Yes, dad, what is it?"

"Now, don't be nervous, son. Just do your best, and if it doesn't work out just remember your mother is going to come to live with you and your wife!"

* * *

A man whose parents had died at an early age went to see a specialist to see if he could improve his own longevity. The specialist told him that although the formula for a long life was unusual, he should try it. The secret was that he had to sprinkle a little gunpowder on his porridge every morning.

The man did this and lived to ninety-eight.

When he died, he left six children, twenty-four grandchildren, fifty-six great-grandchildren, and a twenty-foot hole in the wall of the crematorium.

* * *

The old lady was at the doctor.

"Sorry, but I've got bad news for you, Jessie," said the doctor kindly. "You could go at any time."

"Great, doctor! Ah havenae gone for five days."

* * *

The Scot went to the doctor for his annual check-up. Afterwards the doc said, "The best advice I can give you is to stop drinking a bottle of whisky every night, stop smoking, keep away from naughty women and always make sure you are in bed by midnight."

"An' whit's yer second best advice?"

* * *

"Doctor, if ah have this operation will ah be able tae play ma bagpipes later this month?"

"I cannot guarantee it will be bagpipes," replied the surgeon, "but certainly some instrument. The last time I performed this operation the patient was playing a harp within a week."

* * *

"Quick, Tam. Phone the hospital. Ah'm havin' contractions every ten minutes."

"Hey, jist haud on. Why can't you phone the hospital yersel'. Efter aw, yer doing nothing between contractions, are you?"

* * *

On a farm in Scotland a Highland Cattle bull, an Aberdeen Angus bull and a chicken were arguing as to who was the most fearsome creature in the country.

"When I charge across a field at a group of ramblers they are terrified and run off screaming," said the Highland Cattle bull.

"Listen," said the Aberdeen Angus bull, "when I roar people shake for miles around."

"That's nothing," said the chicken. "When I cough the whole of Scotland craps itself!"

EDUCATION

The teacher asked Wullie if he knew his numbers.

"Aye, ma faither taught me, miss."

"Good. So what comes after four?"

"Five, miss."

"What comes after seven?"

"Eight, miss."

"Seems like your father's done a good job. So, finally, what comes after ten?"

"Jack, miss."

***

The teacher was giving her pupils a lesson in logic.

"Right, I want you to imagine the following situation," she said. "A man is standing up in a boat in the middle of a Scottish river, fishing. He loses his balance, falls into the water then splashes about shouting for help. His wife hears all the commotion, knows he can't swim, and runs to the bank. What does she do?"

A wee girl raised her hand. "Draw oot aw his money, miss?"

***

The university lecturer was discussing the anatomy of males in various Scottish clans. He went on to say, "The men of the McEwan Clan of Mull are commonly acknowledged to be the best endowed."

One female student at the back decided she had had enough and headed for the door at the back of the lecture room.

The lecturer called out, "There's no need to hurry, dear. The next boat to Mull doesn't leave Oban until eight o'clock tomorrow morning."

***

"It's nae good, miss," said the wee fella to his English teacher. "Ah try tae learn, but everything you say just goes in both ears and oot the other."

"Goes in both ears and out the other?" asked the puzzled teacher. "But you only have two ears."

"There, you see, sir. Ah'm nae good at sums, either."

***

A teacher entered her classroom and immediately noticed a pool of water beside the blackboard. "And just who is responsible for this? Ok, I will get the janitor to clean it up and then we will get down to the sorry business of finding out who did it."

Once the janitor had cleaned up, the teacher said, "Now, I want whoever did this to own up. So we will all close our eyes and then the guilty person must come forward and write his or her name on the blackboard."

All closed their eyes and then footsteps were heard approaching the blackboard. After a slight delay there came the scratching of chalk, then the footsteps retreating.

"Right everyone," said the teacher. "You may open your eyes again."

There beside the blackboard was another pool of water, while on the blackboard was written, 'The phantom piddler strikes again!'

"Sorry ah'm late, miss," said Rory to the teacher. "Ye see, ah had tae make ma ain breakfast."

"Never mind, Rory," said the teacher. "Today we are doing Scottish geography. Can anybody tell me where the Scottish border is?"

"Aye, miss," replied Rory. "In bed wi ma mammy. That's why ah had tae make ma ain breakfast."

***

"Why did you get a 'Fail' in your arithmetic test, Willie," asked his father.

"Well the teacher asked me what 3 plus 3 was, and I said 6."

"Quite correct," said his father.

"Then she asked what 4 plus 2 was."

"What's the bleedin' difference?" asked the father.

"That's whit ah said, dad!"

***

The English teacher in a Scottish Secondary School wrote on her blackboard the words:

'A woman without her man is nothing.'

Then she instructed them to punctuate it.

All the boys wrote: 'A woman, without her man, is nothing.'

All the girls wrote: 'A Woman: Without her, man is nothing.'

***

"Listen, Susan," said the teacher. "What in the world is wrong with you? Everything you do and everything you say is wrong! What are you possibly going to do when you leave school?"

"Be a weather girl on BBC Scotland, miss."

***

The science teacher asked her pupils to bring one electrical gadget to school the following day for a 'Show and Learn' session.

The following day the teacher asked Catherine what she had brought.

"I've brought an electrical can opener, miss."

"Very good. Now Isabella, what have you brought?"

"I've brought an iPod, miss. You can download music from the internet with it."

"Excellent. Now Billy, what have you brought?"

"It's just outside the door, miss. It's a heart and lung ventilator from the hospital."

"Goodness, gracious", said the teacher. "And what did your father say about you bringing it to school?"

"He just said, 'AAAAAARRRRRRRGGGGGGH!'"

***

The physics teacher was testing her class for the forthcoming exam.

"Who can tell me what's inertia?"

"Please miss, Prestwick, Troon and Saltcoats."

***

The primary teacher had to leave the classroom for a few minutes. When she returned, she found the children all sitting up, arms folded, perfectly quiet.

She was absolutely stunned. "My goodness," she said. "I've never seen anything like this before. It's wonderful. What's come over you all? Why are you suddenly all so well behaved?"

Wee Fiona at the front put her hand up. "Dae ye no' remember, miss, tellin' us that if you ever came back and found us all quiet, you wid drop deed!"

***

"Today we are going to try our hand at poetry," the teacher informed the class. "I want you to compose a poem about your ambitions in life, and then read it out to the class."

First to give his poem was the class swot.

"My name is Dan,
And when I'm a man,
I would like to visit China and Japan."

Next was the teacher's pet.

"My name is Mary Grady,
And when I become a lady,
I would like to have a baby."

Then came the class tearaway.

"I too am Dan,
But stuff China and Japan,
If Mary Grady wants a baby,
Then ah'm the very man!"

***

The teacher was wandering around her primary class looking at her pupils' drawing efforts.

She came to wee Tommy's table and noticed that his paper was blank.

"What have you drawn, Tommy?"

"A coo, miss."

"And what is your cow doing, Tommy?"

"Eatin' the cud, miss."

"So where is the grass?"

"The coo has eaten it all up, miss."

"And for that matter where is the cow, Tommy?"

"Ye don't think the coo wid be sae daft as tae stay in that field efter she had eaten aw the cud, miss."

***

It was Parents' Night at the school.

"How's oor wee Brian gettin' on?" asked his father.

"Well," said the teacher, "Brian's in a class of his own."

"Great. I didnae know he was that clever."

"He's not. He smells!"

***

Miss Docherty was explaining to her primary class about magnetism. She showed them a magnet and how it would pick up nails and paper clips.

The following day she thought she would do a bit of revision. "Right, children. My name begins with the letter 'M' and I pick up things. What am I?"

A hand went up at the front. "Please, miss," said wee Harry. "A mummy."

***

The toddler sat on the seat in the supermarket trolley as the middle-aged lady pushed it through Tesco in Edinburgh.

Every time she put something in the trolley, she would say, "And here's something for our lunch, Diploma." Or, "Would you like some sweets, Diploma?"

Another shopper overheard this and asked, "I must ask you. Why do you call this little toddler Diploma?"

"Easy. I sent my daughter to St Andrews University and this is what she came home with!"

***

"Dad, you're a clever person. Can you sign your name without opening your eyes?"

"Sure, son."

"Great. Here's a pen. Close yer eyes an' sign ma report card."

It was the day before the holidays and the teacher put two baskets of treats on a table at the front of the class. One contained biscuits, the other pancakes.

"Now children," she told her primary class. "You may only take one treat."

Next to the basket of chocolate biscuits she put up a sign saying, 'Take only one. God is watching.'

As one wee girl reached out to take a pancake the wee boy next to her whispered. "Take all you want. God's watching the biscuits!"

***

On the first day of the term at a Scottish university the principal addressed the students.

"We have strict out-of-bounds rules here. The female halls of residence will be out-of-bounds to all male students, and the male halls of residence to female students. Anybody caught breaking this rule will be fined twenty pounds the first time."

He continued, "Anybody breaking this rule a second time will be fined fifty pounds, and anybody caught breaking this rule a third time, one hundred pounds. Now, are there any questions?"

A male voice came from the crowd. "How much for a season ticket?"

***

The Scots history teacher was explaining the history of Britain to his class.

"You see, boys and girls, the Angles first arrived in Northumberland. The acute Angles turned north and became Scots, but the obtuse Angles turned south and became English."

***

"Under new guidelines," said the teacher, "I must instruct you about a number of various sexual preferences. So, to start off with, who can tell me what a transvestite is? Yes, Jimmy."

"A man that changes his simmit every night, miss?"

***

"Right," said the teacher to her class. **"Let's see how good you are on trade and industry in our country. Who can give me, for any one year, the approximate number of bottles of whisky exported from Scotland?"**

"Please miss, 587AD. None!"

***

"Mum, ah don't want to go to school today."

"Why not, son?"

"Well, two weeks ago the jannie was cleaning out the chicken run in the wee school farm and found a dead one, so we had chicken soup for our school lunch the next day. Then just last week, the jannie was in the wee school farm and found one of the piglets had died, and the following day we had bacon for our school lunch."

"But why don't you want to go to school today, son?"

"The jannie died yesterday."

***

The unmarried teacher entered her classroom, and there on the blackboard was a drawing of a penis.

"Immature nonsense!" she said as she rubbed it off.

The following morning, there again, was another, larger, drawing of a penis.

"Stupid, immature nonsense!" she ranted as she rubbed it off.

The following morning when she came into the class, there was a huge drawing of a penis on the blackboard. Underneath it was a message.

'The more you rub the bigger it gets!'

HOW THE OTHER HALF LIVE!

It was Christmas, and the lady lost her purse in the hustle and bustle of Argyle Street in Glasgow.

A wee boy found it and returned it to her. Looking in her purse she commented, "That's odd. When I lost my bag there was a twenty pound note in it. Now there are two tenners."

"Aye, missus, that's right. Ye see the last time ah found a wumman's purse she didnae huv ony change fur the reward."

***

A social worker went to see a single woman with seventeen children, all boys.

"And what names have you given to your boys?" asked the social worker.

"Ah've called them aw Jimmy," replied the woman.

"Every one of them Jimmy? And what if they are all out playing and you want them in for their tea?"

"Och, ah jist open the door an' shout, 'Jimmy!'"

"But," enquired the social worker, "what if you just want one in, how do you do that?"

"Och, ah jist open the door an' use his surname."

***

"Did ye hear that wee Phyllis is getting merrit?"

"Didnae even know she wis pregnant!"

***

Granny was complaining about the cost of living. "See when ah wis a girl, ah could go out with threepence and come back with two loaves, a dozen eggs, two pints of milk, a pound of cheese, and ten Woodbine for ma fether."

"Aye," said her grandson, "that's inflation for you."

"It's nothing tae dae wi inflation," said granny. "It's aw they security cameras they huv noo!"

***

The barman turned to the drinker at the bar. "Yer a stranger in these parts, eh?"

"How do you know that?"

"Ye keep takin' yer hand aff yer glass."

***

"How's yer sex life, Jimmy?"

"Och, ah'm oan Social Security sex."

"Whit's that?"

"A wee bit each month, but it's no' enough tae live on."

***

A girl sobbed as she confessed to her father that she was pregnant.

"And who is the faither?" screamed her dad.

"How wid ah know," said the girl. "Ye never let me go steady wi' onybuddy."

***

"Where's Big Sammy?" a drinker was asked in a Glasgow pub.

"He started a business building totally unique cars."

"Amazing! What did he do?"

"Well, he took the engine oot o' a Roller, the radiator from a Merc, the seats from a Ferrari, the wheels from a Jag and the chassis from a Volvo."

"So, what did he end up with?"

"Five years in Barlinnie."

***

One night a chap was going through a certain part of Glasgow when he was accosted by a beautiful woman.

"I'll do anything you want for forty pounds," she said, "provided you can ask for it in just three words."

"Paint ma hoose!"

***

Two wee lads were talking.

"Ma new dad's called George," said the first boy.

"Och, he's no good," said the second. "Ah had him last month."

***

"Will the father be present during the birth?" asked the maternity nurse.

"Naw," came the reply. "Ye see, him an' ma man don't get on."

***

The police patrolmen approached the car they had just pulled over. They were surprised to see the driver smacking a dog sitting in the front passenger seat.

When asked to stop hitting the dog the driver

replied. "He's a naughty boy, officer. He's just eaten ma tax disc."

***

A wee woman in Greenock was charged with shooting her husband using a bow and arrow.

At her trial the prosecuting lawyer asked her, "Now tell the court, madam. Why did you shoot your husband using a bow and arrow?"

"Ah didnae want tae wake the weans!"

***

The two work-shy guys were sitting in a pub in Airdrie, spending their Giros. "Ah wis readin' that in Africa," said one guy, "there's a place where there are diamonds all o'er the ground. All you've got tae dae is bend doon an' pick them up."

"Bend doon!"

***

An undertaker in Glasgow was going into his premises when he was accosted by a man. "Dae youse dae funerals?" the man asked.

"Yes, I do," said the undertaker.

"Well, ma auld faither is jist aboot deed."

"Sorry to hear that," said the undertaker politely.

"Ye see he doesnae have ony life insurance or anything."

"Right. So how can ah help?"

"Dae ye dae homers?"

***

A referendum on the Euro was recently held in a town in Scotland. Most people voted to retain the Giro!

***

"How did ye get oan wi' the shopliftin' the day?" the mother asked her wee boy.

"No' very weel, Ma."

"An' whit did ye nick?"

"Two brochures an' a wee pen oot o' Argos."

***

It was the wee boy's first day at school.

"How did ye get oan?" asked his mother.

"Och, ah wish ah hudnae goad."

"Listen, it's no' 'ah wish ah hudnae goad'. It's 'ah wish ah hudnae went'."

"Well, ah wish tae goad ah hudnae went!"

***

What is the difference between a police arrest and a citizen's arrest in Glasgow?

During a citizen's arrest, you do not always suffer the same searing pain in your groin!

***

"Freezin' weather, intit?" said the man to his pal. "Ah canny get warm, even in bed. How dae ye keep warm?"

"Och, ah treated masell tae wan o' they old fashioned bed-warmers."

"A sort of hot-water bottle?"

"Naw, naw. A sixty-nine-year-old granny frae Cumbernauld!"

***

There was a letter in the post to the Scot from his credit company. It said 'Final Notice'.

'Thank heavens that's the last I'll hear frae that lot!"

A Scot got off the plane from Amsterdam, at Glasgow airport. As he was coming through Customs he was stopped and the customs officer asked him, "Spirits, cigarettes or drugs, sir?"

"Naw, it's aw right, pal. Ah've goat plenty."

***

Big Ian came home from the Glasgow Barras with bruised knuckles.

"How did that happen?" asked his wife.

"Ah stopped at a stall selling wood, and the fella asked me if ah needed decking. So ah just got ma retaliation in first!"

***

A young lady went into the Royal Bank of Scotland and dumped a bucket of fifty pence pieces on the counter. The teller buzzed for the supervisor, who then berated the young woman for hoarding so many fifty pence pieces.

The young woman replied. "That's no' fair. Ah didnae hoard all of these. Ma big sister whored half, an' ah only whored the other half!"

***

The wee lad of three was playing with his testicles.

"Hey maw, ur them ma brains?" he asked his mother.

"No' yet, son."

***

The new mother got out of bed for the first time since the birth and walked down the corridor in the hospital to the nurses' desk. "Could ah look at a phone book?" she asked.

"What are you doing out here? You should be in bed resting," a nurse exclaimed.

"Ah want tae search through the phone book fur a name fur ma wean," the new mother replied.

"You don't have to do that. The hospital provides a booklet for all new mothers to assist them in picking a name for their baby."

"You don't understaun," the woman said and frowned. "Ma wean already has a first name."

***

"See this nonsense o' the rubbish only being collected wance a fortnight. Well, ma man has solved the problem."

"How does he dae that?"

"Och, he just wraps it in gift paper, loads it in the back o' his wee car and parks it in Glesca. It's gone in five minutes!"

***

The Glasgow hypnotist was treating a wee boy patient for kleptomania.

"You are now cured. You will not steal anymore. However, should you relapse, see if you can get me wan o' they forty-two inch high-definition flat screen tellies."

***

The mother and father were sitting drinking on the couch in their living room while they watched their children playing.

"Who the hell taught oor children tae swear like that?" asked the father.

"Ah'm damned if ah know," replied the mother.

***

Siamese twins from Glasgow decided to write their autobiography. They called it 'Oor Wullie'.

***

A Scot, steamin' and skint, is walking down Argyle Street when he spots a guy tinkering with the engine of his car.

"Whit's up, pal?" he asks.

"Piston broke," came the reply.

"Aye, same as masel'!"

***

The loan shark was giving a customer a loan. "Understaun," he said. "It's a Personal loan. That means ye've goat tae keep up the payments."

"An' whit if ah don't?"

"That's when ah get personal!"

***

Two wives were talking.

"Do you think it is a good idea to kiss your children goodnight?" asked one of the wives.

"Aye, it is," replied the other. "That is, if you don't mind waiting up till they get home."

***

A man is driving through a certain Scottish town when his car splutters to a halt. He puts up the bonnet and looks around the engine compartment. Then he hears a noise from the rear of the car. There he sees a wee boy with a crowbar trying to lever open the boot. "Hey! This is ma car!" shouts the man.

"Keep yer hair on big man," shouts the wee fellow. "You dae the front half, I'll dae the back."

The guy was in Princes Street selling the Big Issue.

"Help the homeless," he shouted. "Buy the Big Issue."

A businessman stopped, fumbled in his pocked and discovered he had no money. "Sorry," he said, "but if you give me a copy I'll tell you a joke."

"OK."

"Right. Knock, knock!"

"Who's there?"

"Don't know."

"See. You're not homeless at all!"

***

Wally went into an ironmongers shop. "Gizza bottle o' meth."

"Get lost," said the shopkeeper, "you'll just drink it."

"Naw me, pal," says Wally. "Go on, gizz wan bottle o' meth."

"I told you. You can't have one. You'll just drink it."

"Honest injun. Ah promise ah won't."

"Awright, then. Here's wan. That'll be a pound," said the shopkeeper taking a bottle off a shelf.

"Any chance o' wan oot the fridge?"

POLITICIANS ... PLUS PEOPLE WHO WORK!

"May I ask you a personal question, First Minister," asked the BBC reporter. "How old are you?"

"Fifty-two."

"But, First Minister, that is what you said two years ago."

"Aye, but I always stand by what I say."

***

"Daddy, do all fairy tales start with 'Once upon a time'?"

"No, dear. Some start with 'When I am elected'."

***

"Now," said the interviewer, "before we start the interview I would like you to take an intelligence test."

"Intelligence test!" said the applicant. "Your advert said nothing about an intelligence test. It just stated you were looking for an assistant for an MSP."

***

The little old Scotsman, dressed in a kilt, made his way down Whitehall in London, stopping at the gates of Downing Street. There he spoke to the policeman on duty. "Can ah please speak tae Tony Blair?"

"Sorry, sir," replied the policeman, "Tony Blair is no longer the Prime Minister."

The following day the same old Scot arrived at the gates of Downing Street and asked the same policeman, "Can ah please speak tae Tony Blair?"

"Sorry, sir," replied the policeman, "but I think I told you Tony Blair is no longer the Prime Minister."

The next day the same Scot arrived again at the gates of Downing Street and asked the same policeman. "Can ah please speak tae Tony Blair?"

"Sir! I have told you that Tony Blair is no longer the Prime Minister. Why do you keep asking me?"

"Because ah jist love tae hear ye saying it!"

***

The maths professor at Edinburgh University stood before his class and posed a question.

"Just suppose," he said, "that a wealthy laird in the Highlands died leaving an estate of fifty-one million pounds. One third to go to his wife, one fifth to his son, one sixth to his daughter, one eighth to his secretary, and one ninth to his butler. Now, what does each get?"

A student immediately raised his hand. "A good lawyer!"

***

Two men got to talking in a pub on the Royal Mile in Edinburgh.

"So, do you work near here?" asked one fellow.

"Yes, I work at the Scottish Parliament."

"Are you an MSP, then?"

"No, no. I'm a Logic Analyst."

"And what in the world does a Logic Analyst do?"

"Oh, we work on the logic of proposed bills going through the Parliament. Logic can explain anything in this world, you know," said the Logic Analyst. "Let me explain in simple terms. Do you have a goldfish at home?"

"As it happens, I do."

"Well, it's logical to assume you keep it in a bowl or a pond. Which is it?"

"It's in a pond."

"Then it is logical to assume you have a large garden?"

"Yes, I've got a large garden."

"And if you have a large garden it is logical to assume you have a large house."

"Yes, I've got a large five bedroomed house. In fact I built it myself."

"Given that you've built a five bedroomed house it is logical to assume you haven't built it for yourself, and that you are quite probably married."

"Yes, I'm married and have four children."

"Then it is logical that you are sexually active with your wife on a regular basis."

"At least four times a week."

"Then it is logical that you do not masturbate very often."

"Me? Never."

"There you are then. From finding out if you have a goldfish, I've told you about your sex life."

"Very impressive. Thanks for explaining logic to me."

The following day the man was talking to a pal and telling him about meeting the Logic Analyst from the Scottish Parliament.

"So, how does it work?" asked his pal.

"Well, do you have a goldfish?"

"Naw."

"Then you're a wanker."

The Scottish First Minister phoned the British Prime Minister. "What's this about you sending an Englishman into space?"

"Oh, don't worry. Next time we will send a Scotsman."

"Oh, you don't understand, Prime Minister. I wasn't complaining. On the contrary I congratulate you. But why stop at one?"

***

Tony Blair and his driver were cruising along a Highland road one night when all of a sudden they hit a pig, killing it instantly.

Tony told his driver to go to the nearby farmhouse and explain to the owners what had happened.

An hour later the driver staggered back to the car with an almost empty bottle of malt whisky in one hand, a box of cigars in his other hand and his clothes somewhat dishevelled.

"What happened to you?" asked Tony.

"Well the farmer insisted I drank his whisky, his wife gave me this box of cigars, and his nineteen-year-old daughter made mad passionate love to me."

"For heavens sake, man. What in the world did you tell them?"

"Well, sir, all I told them was that I was Tony Blair's driver, and I had just killed the pig."

***

A departmental manager in a large firm in Edinburgh asked the new employee, sent to him by the Personnel Department, what his name was.

"Allister."

"Let us get this straight, right at the start. I don't go in for all this business of using first names. It does nothing but breed familiarity and can lead to a breakdown in authority. I always refer to my employees by their surnames only. You will call me Mister Smith. Now what is your name?"

"Darling. Allister Darling."

"Ok Allister, the next thing I have got to tell you is . . ."

***

A customer in a Scottish bank was served, moved away from the teller and counted his money.

"Hey, you've given me the wrong money," said the customer.

"Sorry, sir," replied the teller, "but you have moved away from the counter. We don't change anything after you leave. It's bank policy."

"Fair enough, pal," said the customer. "Ah just though ah would let you know you gave me an extra hundred pounds. Cheerio!"

***

A motorist in the Highlands drove behind a truck and flashed his lights. The truck stopped.

The motorist got out of his car and went over to the truck.

"Just to let you know," said the motorist, "that you are losing some of your load."

"Well," said the driver of the truck, "you may have noticed that it is a freezing cauld night here in the Highlands, so ah'm gritting the roads!"

***

A man went to Glasgow Council for a job interview.

The interviewer asked, "Have you been in the armed services?"

"Yes," he says, "I was in Iraq."

"Are you disabled in any way?"

"Yes," said the interviewee, "I was holding a grenade and it went off and I lost both of my thumbs."

The interviewer said, "Okay. You're hired. Start on Monday. The hours are 8am to 4.30pm. However you can come in at 10am."

The chap was puzzled, "Thanks for hiring me but why do I not need to start till 10am if the hours are 8am till 4.30pm?"

"Well, you see," replied the interviewer, "this is a Council job and there is no point in your coming in early. All we do for the first couple of hours is twiddle our thumbs."

***

A Highlander wanted a loan of £200 so he went to a bank. He was interviewed by the bank manager.

"What do you wish the loan for?" asked the manager.

"Tae tak ma sheep tae merket in Eberdeen tae sell them."

"What do you have in the way of collateral?" queried the banker.

"And jist whit does collateral mean?" asked the Highlander.

"Well, it's something of value that would cover the amount of the loan."

"Ah've a 1958 Bedford truck."

"How about livestock."

"Jist the sheep ah want tae sell and an auld cuddy."

"How old is your horse?"

"Ah dinna ken. He doesna huv ony teeth."

"OK," said the banker, somewhat reluctantly. "You can have the loan."

Two weeks later the Highlander was back in the bank. He pulled out a pile of notes, took some, and said, "Here's the money to pay the loan," and handed over the amount plus the interest.

"And what are you going to do with the rest of that wad of money?" asked the banker.

"Pit it in ma pocket."

"Why don't you deposit it in this bank?"

"And jist what does deposit mean?"

"Well, you put the money in the bank and we take care of it."

The old Highlander leaned across the desk, looked suspiciously at the banker, and asked, "What do you have in the way of collateral?"

***

A chartered accountant in Edinburgh was accosted by a vagrant, who asked, "Ony spare change?"

"And if I did have, why should I give it to you?" asked the accountant.

"Fur the simple reason ah'm doon on ma luck. Ah've lost ma job and ma wife and six children are starving. Ah don't have a penny to feed them."

"I see. And how does that compare with the corresponding quarter last year?"

***

Two Scottish farmers were boasting about the strongest winds they'd encountered.

"On ma farm in Aberdeenshire," said one, "we had one of the strongest gales ever. Ma coos were blown from one end of the field to the other."

"That's nothing," said the other. "Back on ma farm on Islay, we had a terrible storm one day that blew at well over one hundred miles an hour. It was so bad, one of ma hens turned her back tae the wind and laid the same egg six times."

***

The RAF pilot was flying his Tornado over the North

Sea when he noticed on his port side a man sitting on a carpet with a machine gun. Glancing to his starboard side he saw another man on a carpet with a machine gun. Feeling threatened, he did a loop and machine-gunned both carpets out of the sky.

On arrival back at the base in Lossiemouth he was immediately summoned to see the commander.

"You are in big trouble," said the commander. "We saw on radar what you did."

"What do you mean, sir? I shot these threatening carpets down."

"Yes, but they were Allied Carpets!"

***

The MSP was handed a letter by his secretary that had arrived in the post.

The letter contained only one word: 'Bastard'.

"What do you think of that?" asked the secretary.

"Well, I've received plenty of letters where the writer hadn't signed it, but this is the first time someone has signed the letter and forgotten to write it."

***

The manager in a large Edinburgh insurance company wondered how one of the clerks was able to afford his large house in Morningside and drive a Rolls Royce, on a salary of a thousand pounds a month.

Finally he asked the employee who said, "It's easy. I sell five thousand raffle tickets a month at five pounds each."

"And what are you raffling?"

"My salary."

***

The little old lady stood outside the polling station on election day. One of the bystanders asked her, "Who did you vote for?"

Said the little old lady, "I never vote. It only encourages them."

***

Terrorists seized control of the Scottish Parliament Building. If their demands were not met they threatened to release an MSP every hour!

***

A chap decided to apply to a political party to be considered as a candidate for the Scottish Parliament.

As the man was unknown to the selection committee, he was given a confidential, sealed envelope and told to deliver it to the party chairman in his office in another part of the building.

Outside the party chairman's office the fellow looked around, nobody was in sight, so he opened the envelope. It read, 'Congratulations! You are our kind of person. Now go in and see the party chairman.'

***

A Highlander was travelling on a train across the north of Scotland. A young man across from him asked, "Excuse me, what time is it?" The Highlander said nothing. Again the young man asked, "What time is it?" Still the Highlander said nothing. Again the young man asked, "Can you tell me the time? Why don't you answer me?"

"Listen, son," said the Highlander. "We are jist about to come to the terminus on this route. I don't know you, so you are a stranger. If I answer you I will have to extend Highland hospitality to you. Och, I would need to invite you to ma home. I have a lovely daughter. You

might both fall in love and want to get married. So, tell me, why would I need a son-in-law who cannae even afford a watch?"

***

The Scottish stockbroker was sitting at a hotel bar in Edinburgh. A very attractive young lady came over and sat beside him. "Wid ye like some company, mister?"

"Perhaps. What was the net profit last year?"

***

After twenty-five years in the same parish a priest was being honoured by his parishioners with a special dinner. Many important people had been invited.

Before the meal the priest was invited to say a few words.

"Ladies and gentleman, unfortunately I got my initial impression of this parish from the first confession I heard here. I thought the Bishop had assigned me to a terrible place. This man told me that he had stolen money from his parents, had affairs with five married women, had incestuous relationships, had taken many bribes and backhanders, and had used and sold drugs. I was appalled. But as the days went on, I learned that the people here were not all like that, and indeed this parish is really made up of warm and caring people."

Just as the priest finished his talk, the local MSP arrived full of apologies for being late. He immediately got to his feet to give his speech.

"Ladies and gentlemen, I'll never forget the day our new parish priest arrived. In fact I had the honour of being the first person to go to him for confession."

***

The young lassie was in the branch of a bank requesting a loan.

"Do you have any money in the bank?" asked the manager.

"Aye. Ah dae."

"How much?"

"Ah dinnae ken. Ah huvnae shaken it recently."

***

The First Minister announced that to be fair to the total population of Scotland, he was putting forward a bill whereby all Scottish towns must have two swimming pools. One would be full of water. The other empty.

"Empty? Whit fur?" asked the opposition spokesperson.

"For people who can't swim!"

***

A surgeon and his wife were attending a dinner-party in Edinburgh. Their host, a somewhat boastful man, was carving the meat.

"So, how am I doing, doc? Look at these neat slices. Do you like my technique. Don't you think I would make a pretty good surgeon?"

"Pretty good. But let's see you put it back together again!"

***

Jimmie needed to get rid of his old carpet. He put it in his front garden and put a sign on it, 'Free carpet. Help yourself'.

A week went by and the carpet was still there. So Jimmie put a different sign on it. 'For sale . . . £25.'

The next time he looked out the window the carpet had been stolen.

***

A couple were being shown around the new Parliament building in Edinburgh. Their guide pointed out a tall, benevolent fellow as the Parliament's chaplain.

"And what does the chaplain do?" the lady asked. "Does he pray for the MSPs?"

"No, he gets to his feet, looks at the MSPs, and then prays for the country!"

***

The Scots troop had been on field patrols in Afghanistan for a month when the sergeant got them all together. "Listen, lads. We've been away from base for a number of weeks now. I've got good and bad news for you. First the good news. Today we're going to change our underwear." A huge cheer went up.

"Now for the bad news. McPherson, you change with McAlpine, McDougal, you change with McDermid, McLaughlan . . ."

***

The First Minister was addressing the Scottish Parliament. "I want you all to know that when my party took office, Scotland's economy was teetering on the edge of an abyss. I'm proud to say that since then we have made a valiant stride forward."

***

A farmer in the Borders had a clever sheepdog called Accountant. One day the farmer told the sheepdog to go and count the sheep in the field.

When the dog returned the farmer asked, "Right, how many sheep were there in the field?"

The dog replied, "A hundred, farmer."

"That's funny," said the farmer. "I thought there were ninety-nine sheep in that field."

"You're right, farmer. But I rounded them up for you."

***

The junior member of the accountancy firm went to see his manager. "I wonder if I could have a day off next week, please, sur."

"And just why do you want a day off next week, laddie?" asked his manager.

"Ah'm gettin' married, sur."

"Married! But you only earn minimum wage, you're poor at your work, got no prospects, and to be honest I was thinking of letting you go. Who would want to marry someone like you, laddie?"

"Yer daughter, sur."

***

A man was called to appear in front of the local Inland Revenue investigator, so he asked his accountant for advice. "Wear your shabbiest clothes. They will think you are poor."

Then he asked a friend who was an actuary the same question, but got a completely different answer. "Don't be intimidated during this interview. Wear your very best suit."

Confused, the man talked to his lawyer.

"Let me tell you a story," said his lawyer. "A woman, about to be married, asked her mother what to wear on her wedding night. Her mother told her to wear a heavy, flannel nightgown that went from her toes to her neck. But she also asked her best friend who gave her a conflicting answer. She said she should wear her most sexy see-through negligee."

The man protested, "But what does that have to do with my meeting with the Inland Revenue?"

The lawyer replied. "Easy. It doesn't matter what you wear, you're going to get screwed anyway!"

***

The old Scottish industrialist owned a small manufacturing plant with just ten male employees. One day his workers opted to go on a sit-down strike.

The old Scot went to the factory floor and told the strikers that if they were going to have a sit-in they may as well be comfortable, so he provided blankets, pillows and bottles of whisky.

When the whisky was almost consumed the owner arranged for ten young women to entertain the strikers.

Then he got a mini-bus and collected the strikers' wives so that they could be reassured that their husbands were fine.

Five minutes later the strike was over.

***

The Perth woman had only been in the shop for ten minutes, but when she came out there was a traffic warden writing out a parking ticket.

"Come on," she said to the traffic warden, "have you people no shame?"

The traffic warden ignored her and finished writing the ticket. She then stuck it on the windscreen of the BMW.

"You know what you are?" said the woman. "You are a slimy sleazeball. You should have been in the Gestapo. All you want to do is make people's lives a misery."

"Right," exclaimed the traffic warden. "Fur ah that cheek ah'm gonnae give you another fine!" and started to write out another ticket.

"You are the lowest of the low," continued the woman. "Naebuddy in the world could like somebuddy like you. You jist like handin' oot misery tae other folks."

By this time the traffic warden had put the second ticket on the windscreen. She turned and said, "Ah'm fed up wi your attitude. Ah'm only doin' ma public duty. It's posh folks like you that make me sick. So yer getting another ticket!" and she started to write out yet another parking fine.

The woman turned on her heel and was about to walk away, when the traffic warden said, "Hey, where dae you think you're goin'?"

"Roon the corner," came the reply. "That's where ma bus stop is."

***

It was Saturday lunchtime and a dad and his twelve-year-old daughter arrived home after a trip into Aberdeen to get her ears pierced.

When they walked through the door the mother gasped with horror. Her daughter had her ears pierced, a stud through her nose, a bolt in her eyebrows, a ring in her lip and a chain hanging from her cheek to her ear.

"Heavens above. What have you done?"

"Well, you see, the shop had a special offer on."

***

An old couple in Scotland still had their son living at home. They were worried about him, and decided to give him a test to best determine his future.

They left a £50 note and a bottle of malt whisky on the kitchen table. Then they hid awaiting their son's arrival home. The father had calculated that if the son took the money he would either be in business or finance but if he took the whisky he would be a drunk.

The son duly arrived and seeing the money he inserted it in a brown envelope and put it in his pocket. He opened the whisky, sniffed to determine the quality of the malt, and then left the room with both items.

The father turned white with shock and said, "Heavens, it's worse than I thought. He's going to be a MSP!"

***

As the MSPs gathered for First Minister's question time, the speaker shouted out loudly, "Order please, order now!"

One Glasgow MSP immediately replied, "A hauf and a beer!"

***

An elderly Scottish couple celebrated their seventieth anniversary. They had been childhood sweethearts at school. So they decided to visit their old primary school not far from where they lived.

It wasn't locked, and they found the old desk they had shared and where they had carved their initials.

As they slowly walked home, a security van passed and a sack fell out. They took it home, opened it, and there was fifty thousand pounds.

The old man said, "My dear, we will need to give the money back."

"No, no," said his wife. "Finders keepers." And she hid the money in the loft.

The following day two detectives came to the door. They were going round the neighbourhood trying to find the missing money.

"Sorry to bother you, but did either of you find a bag that fell from a security van yesterday?"

The old woman said, "No."

Her husband quickly said, "I'm afraid she is lying. She's hidden it in the loft."

The old woman said, "Don't believe him. He's gone senile."

But one of the detectives started to question the old man. "Now, sir. Just tell us your story from the beginning."

"Well, when my wife and I were coming back from primary school yesterday . . ."

"Sorry to bother you, folks," said the other detective. "We'll try next door."

SCOTS LAW

It was the Sheriff Court in Paisley.

"Now, repeat the words the defendant used," asked the prosecuting lawyer.

"I'd prefer not to," replied the witness. "You see, they're not fit words to tell a gentleman."

"Then whisper them to the sheriff."

***

An attractive policewoman was in a police car when she saw a car swerving all over the road. She signalled to the car to pull over to the side of the road, and a driver, very drunk, fell out the car, got to his feet and made his way unsteadily towards the patrol car.

"You're staggering," said the policewoman.

"Aye, an you're no' so bad yersel', hen."

***

The prosecuting lawyer was cross-examining the murderess.

"And after you poisoned the porridge and your husband sat at breakfast partaking of the fatal cereal, did you not feel any qualms? Did you not feel the slightest pity for this man who had been a good husband to you for thirty years, who was about to die and was totally unaware of it?"

"Well, I suppose there was one moment when I felt a wee bit sorry for him."

"And just when was that?"

"When he asked for a second plateful."

***

Two muggers held up a man in Edinburgh.

"I'm a lawyer," protested the man.

"Right, aff ye go, then," said one of the muggers.

"Hey!" said the other mugger. "Why did ye let him go?"

"Don't be daft. He's wan o' us."

***

An old Scot was driving through rural England when he suddenly hit a calf and killed it. Along came an irate farmer. "Listen, that calf was worth three hundred pounds. In another six years it would have been worth a thousand pounds, so, under English law you owe me one thousand pounds."

The old Scottish motorist duly gave the farmer a cheque for a thousand pounds.

When the farmer presented the cheque to his bank they rejected it. In accordance with Scots law it had been post-dated six years.

***

A man entered a post office in Scotland on the 13th February and saw a fat, balding middle-aged chap with piles of pink envelopes. Each envelope had a heart on it, and as he watched, the man brought out a spray and sprayed them all with a very expensive perfume.

"Excuse me," said the man, "I have just got to ask you what you are doing?"

The chap stopped and said, "I am sending out two thousand Valentine cards."

"Whit! Dae ye fancy yersel' as a right Romeo, then?"

"No, no. I'm a divorce lawyer."

***

"What is your occupation?" asked the sheriff.

"Ah don't have any," replied the defendant. "Ah just sort of circulate around."

"Please note," said the sheriff turning to the clerk of the court, "this gentleman is retired from circulation for sixty days."

***

The defence lawyer was giving his final speech at the end of a murder trial in Glasgow, where the defendant happened to be a gorgeous young lady. He addressed the all male jury.

"Gentlemen, if you find my client guilty she will be taken from this place to a cell in Cornton Vale Prison. Most of her beautiful, blonde hair will be shorn, she will be dressed in a dirty overall and made to do menial tasks for many, many years, before emerging as an old woman. However, if you find my client not guilty, she will return to her luxury flat in the west end of Glasgow, the phone number of which is 0141–143–XXXX."

***

The man was accosted by a detective when he came out of the polling station. "Sir, I am going to arrest you for accepting a bribe and having sold your vote."

"Completely untrue. Ah only voted for ma candidate because I like him."

"We have evidence that you accepted twenty pounds from him."

"Well, it's common sense. If someone gives you twenty pounds, you're going to like them."

***

A Scotsman received a Christmas card from his lawyer with the following message inside.

'Please accept under no obligation, either implied or implicit, my best wishes for the celebration of the winter solstice, as practised by many traditions of the religious persuasion and traditions of others, or on the other hand their choice not to practice religious traditions.

I also wish you a fiscally successful New Year but not without due respect for the calendars of choice for other cultures whose contributions to Scottish society have contributed to our country, without regard to race, creed, colour or sexual preference of choice.

This greeting is subject to clarification or withdrawal and is not freely transferable. Under Scots Law warranty of these good tidings is limited and is at the sole discretion of the wisher. The wishee further agrees to indemnify the wisher, along with their heirs and assignees.

The billing and stamp duty on this document has been calculated at our normal rate. This amounts to fifty pounds which must be received at this office within ten working days otherwise interest at no more than 7% will be added on a monthly basis.'

***

McGonigal, an Edinburgh lawyer, bribed a man on the jury of a murder case in which he was the lawyer for the defence. He wanted the man to influence the jury to bring in a manslaughter verdict rather than one of murder.

After the trial the jury deliberated for many days before bringing out their verdict of manslaughter.

When McGonigal eventually managed to talk to the bent juror, he asked how easy it had been to influence the other jurors.

"Och," said the juror, "ah had a terrible time. The rest o' them wanted to bring in a 'not guilty' verdict."

***

The defence lawyer visited his client in jail. "I've got bad news and good news for you. The blood test you took shows that your DNA matches exactly the DNA found on the victim's clothes."

"And what's the good news?"

"Your cholesterol is down to 3.8."

***

"What is your age?" asked the sheriff. "Now remember madam that you are under oath."

"Thirty-nine and some months."

"How many months?" the sheriff persisted.

"A hundred and twenty!"

***

"Why did you steal the man's personal computer?" asked the sheriff.

"Ah jist took it fur a joke, sur."

"And how far did you carry it?"

"Aboot four miles."

"Nine months in jail. That's carrying a joke too far!"

***

The defendant was on trial for murder. Although there was much evidence against him, no body had been found. His defence lawyer decided that there was only one thing to be done.

"Ladies and gentlemen of the jury," he stated. "I have a surprise for you. In exactly one minute the person presumed dead in this case will walk into this court." He looked towards the doors of the courtroom. The jurors eagerly followed his gaze.

The lawyer then announced: "Forgive me, but I actually made up what I just told you. However you all looked at the door with anticipation. Therefore I put it to you that there exists considerable doubt as to whether anyone was killed, and I ask you to bring in a verdict of 'not guilty'."

The jury retired to deliberate. In five minutes they were back. The verdict was guilty.

"But," inquired the judge, "you must have had some doubt. Even I saw you staring at the door."

The jury foreman replied. "Aye, sur, we did look. But the defendant didn't."

***

Jock went to see his lawyer. "A friend owes me a thousand pounds. He refuses to repay me and even denies borrowing the money from me."

"Do you have any proof he owes you a thousand pounds?" asked the lawyer.

"No, we did it on a handshake."

"Very well," said the lawyer. "I'll write and tell him he owes you ten thousand pounds."

"But I told you he only borrowed a thousand," said the man.

"True," said the lawyer. "And when he writes back to tell me that, we will have him."

TRADITIONAL ONES

The Scot was fined for indecent exposure. Apparently the man had continually wiped the perspiration off his brow with his kilt.

***

Two Scottish ladies were talking in the street. "I didn't know that your young Malcolm had to wear glasses."

"Well, he doesn't have to wear them," explained the other, "but they were his late father's and it seems a pity to waste them."

***

The pipe band was playing in the street and one of their members was doing a door-to-door collection.

One door was opened by a very old Scottish lady.

"I'm collecting for the Inverauchty World Famous District Pipe Band."

"Whit?" she said, holding her hand to her ear.

"I'm collecting for the Inverauchty World Famous District Pipe Band."

"It's nae use, son. Ah cannae hear a word."

The man turned on his heel, muttering, "O' tae hell wi ye."

She immediately replied, "Aye, and tae hell with the Inverauchy World Famous District Pipe Band!"

***

A mother felt she had a cold coming on, so she made herself a hot toddy.

As she was putting her daughter to bed the wee lassie observed, "Mummy! You've been using daddy's aftershave again!"

***

Two old friends were talking.

"Dae ye remember the summer o' 2006?"

"Aye, ah remember it fine."

"Dae ye remember the summer o' 2007?"

"Aye, ah remember it fine, too."

"Dae ye remember the summer o' 2008?"

"Aye, ah remember it fine, as well."

"How come ye remember they summers so well?"

"Well, in the first summer we had a lovely picnic on the beach at North Berwick. On the second summer ah got ma face tanned that afternoon. And on the next one ah spent the whole hour trying tae get aff ma simmit."

***

A Scot in a pub knocked back ten whiskies, one after the other.

"Heavens above," observed the barman. "You fairly drink fast."

"Ah know. Ah once hud wan knocked over."

***

Twenty minutes after the *Titanic* sank, Jamie and Jock find themselves on the same overturned lifeboat. The water is freezing and the boat seems to be sinking.

"Oh, well," said Jamie, "it could have been worse."

"Worse? How could it be worse?"

"We could have bought return tickets."

One of six Aberdeen brothers was sent to America to make his fortune, then come back and share it with the rest. The youngest, Robbie, was selected, and off he went on the plane.

Ten years later he phoned his brothers to say he was coming back. When he got off the plane at Aberdeen airport he couldn't see anyone he knew. Then he was approached by five bearded men.

"Hello, Robbie, dae ye no' recognise yer ain brothers?"

"Goodness gracious, boys, what have ye all grown beards for?"

"We had tae, Robbie. You took the razor wi' ye!"

***

The kilted Scot entered the casino. At one roulette table, two female croupiers were waiting on customers.

"Wid ye mind," asked the Scot, "if ah put ten thousand pounds on ma lucky number seven?"

"No problem whatsoever," answered one of the ladies.

"Aye, an' there's jist wan other thing," said the Scotsman. "Ah find ah'm luckier if ah hide ma face wi ma kilt."

So the wheel was spun, the Scotsman lifted up his kilt and yelled, "Ah've won, ah've won." He picked up the money and left.

The two croupiers were dumfounded. "Did ye see if it landed on number seven?" asked one.

"I don't know," replied the other. "I thought you were watching!"

***

The old chap was very proud of his daughters but was anxious to see them married before he passed away.

One night in the pub he said to the lads, "My

youngest, Kirsty, she's a good looking girl of twenty-five. I'll give her twenty-five thousand pounds when she marries. Then there is Helen who is thirty-nine. When she marries I'll give her thirty-nine thousand pounds. Finally, there's my eldest, Mary who is forty-six. When she marries I'll give her forty-six thousand pounds."

The Scot in the group piped up. "Ye widnae happen tae have wan between sixty and seventy?"

***

The BBC interviewer was doing a programme on the derivations of place names. She stopped a woman in George Street, in Edinburgh.

"Excuse me, madam, but do you know why Edinburgh is so called?"

The reply came, "I'll have you know it is warmer than Glasgow!"

***

"I mended that hole in your trouser pocket after you went to bed last night. Sure ah'm a nice, wee, thoughtful wife, darling?"

"You certainly are, my wee precious. But tell me, how did you discover there was a hole in my pocket?"

***

"Will you marry me. Yes or no?"
"No."
"Sure?"
"Aye."
"Waiter, divide the bill in two."

***

"I wonder, Mister Kinloch," began the timid young man. "Er . . . will you . . . will you . . ."

"Of course," said Mister Kinloch. "You may have her."

"Sorry, Mister Kinloch," answered the young man, "I don't understand. Have whom?"

"My daughter, of course. You want to marry her, don't you?"

"No. I just wanted to know if you would lend me a pound?"

"A pound? Certainly not! Why, I hardly know you."

***

The woman was the last of six Scottish sisters to marry. The confetti was filthy.

***

Two burglars broke into a house in Glasgow. They were discovered and a tremendous fight broke out. Bleeding and covered in bruises they just managed to escape.

"Well," said one burglar, "At least we didnae do too badly. We came away with fifty quid."

"Aye," said the other one. "But we went in wi' over a hundred!"

***

"Yes, what do you want?" asked the lady of the house to the stranger at the door.

"I want to see your husband about a bill . . ."

"Oh! He left yesterday to go into Perth . . ."

". . . I have to pay your husband."

". . . and from which he returned an hour ago."

***

"After all yer wee tiffs wi' Jeanie, ah hear you have still decided to go through with the wedding."

"Aye. She's pit oan so much weight that she couldna get ma engagement ring aff!"

***

The Englishman was in court, charged with drunkenness. The sheriff asked him where he had bought the alcohol?

"But I didn't buy it, sir," he told the sheriff. "A Scotsman gave it to me."

"Fourteen days for perjury," said the sheriff.

***

"That's a fine looking hat you're wearing," said one Scot to another.

"Aye, I bought it twenty years ago, changed it twice in church and three times in restaurants, and it's still as good as new."

***

Some Scottish Questions:

Q. What do you call a dwarf in Scotland who falls into a cement mixer?

A. A wee hard man!

Q. What do you call a man in Scotland who takes a small size in a shoe?

A. Wee Shooey!

Q. What do you call a man in Scotland who takes a small size in a shoe and doesn't have a dog?

A. Wee Shooey Douglas.

Q. What did Dracula get when he came to Glasgow?

A. A bat in the mooth!

Q. If there are two coos in a field in Scotland, which one is on its holidays?

A. The wan wi the wee calf!

Q. Why was the Scottish diver stupid?

A. He didnae have a scubee!

***

The guide was talking to a visitor to Scotland. "Scotland is a land of inventors. We practically invented everything you can think of, except of course, the toothbrush."

"Oh, where was the toothbrush invented?" asked the visitor.

"England. If we had invented it we would have called it the teethbrush!"

***

The wedding vows had been thought out by the couple themselves. They had promised to 'be married for as long as we feel good about each other'.

At the reception one lady was talking to a friend from Aberdeen. "And what, if I may ask did you get them as a wedding present?"

"Paper cups and plates," came the reply.

***

Angus was on his honeymoon in Paris when he met one of his friends from Scotland.

"Where's yer wife, Angus? I thought you were on honeymoon."

"Och, I am. She's back home in Edinburgh. She's been to Paris before."

***

The Scot went to have his suit dry-cleaned. The assistant said it would cost twenty pounds. The Scot thought that too dear so he went to the charity shop next door and donated the suit.

Three days later he went back into the charity shop after the suit had been cleaned and bought it for five pounds.

***

The old lady stopped a couple in the street in Inverness. "I just have to tell you that it is so nice to see a man and woman always holding hands. I have been watching you both for the last hour or so and you seem to hold hands all the time."

The husband replied. "You're right. If I let go, she shops."

***

The cinema manager in the Odeon in Aberdeen made a public announcement. "Will the person who lost a wallet containing two hundred pounds please form a double queue at the ticket office."

***

The thrifty old Scot lived in a huge mansion in London. A thief thought that it would be an ideal place to burgle.

When he entered the mansion one night he found a safe. A notice on the door said, 'Please do not use dynamite. This safe is not locked. Just turn the lock.'

He did so. Instantly a heavy sandbag fell on him, the entire premises were floodlit and alarms clanged all over the house.

As the police helped him into the patrol car, he was heard moaning, "See them Scots!"

***

"Hello, this is Willie."

"Hi, Willie. What's on yer mind?"

"I've broken down on the M8 and I need two hundred pounds right away."

"There must be something wrong with this line. I can't hear you."

"I said I want to borrow two hundred pounds."

"I can't hear a word you are saying."

"Hello. This is the operator. I can hear your party very plainly."

"Fine. Then you give him two hundred pounds."

***

Sandy hobbled into a bar in Inverness and sat beside his pal, Jock.

Jock asked. "What's your problem, Sandy? You look terrible."

"Och, it's just yoorz. I've a terrible bout of yoorz."

"Whit's yoorz?"

"A double malt, thank you."

***

The United Cooperative Bakery Society building was situated in Clydebank. It had a large chimney with UCBS in very large letters on it.

During the Clydebank Blitz most of Clydebank was razed to the ground but the chimney stood.

When the Luftwaffe bombers got back to Germany after their final night's bombing the captain of one of the aircraft was debriefed by his commander.

"Vell, Kapitan. Vat are your observations after tonight's mission?"

"Commander, Germany vill not vin the war."

"And just vhy not?" demanded the commander.

"The large chimney with UCBS still stands."

"Ha, so?"

"Apparently it means, 'You Cannae Beat Scotland!'"

***

The usher was passing around a collection plate at the large church wedding. One of the guests looked up, puzzled. Without waiting for the question, the usher nodded his head, "I know it's unusual, but the father of the bride requested it."

***

At an Old Firm match a spectator found himself in the thick of flying bottles.

"There's nothing tae worry aboot, pal," said an elderly chap sitting next to him. "It's just like in the war. You won't get hit unless the bottle's got your name on it."

"That's just what worries me," said the fan. "Ma name's Johnnie Walker."

***

After she woke up, a woman told her husband, "I just had a wonderful dream. I dreamed that you gave me a beautiful, expensive necklace for my birthday. What do you think it means?"

"You'll know tonight," he said, and winked.

That evening, the man came home with a small package and gave it to his wife. Delighted, she opened it. It was a book entitled, 'How to Interpret Your Dreams.'

***

The English General got a case of cold feet just before the battle of Prestonpans against the Highlanders.

"Right, men," he said. "I'm afraid we are going to be beaten, lads. But you must fight as bravely as you can. If the worst comes to the worst, run for it. As for me, I'm a bit lame, so I'll start now."

***

"Dad, I'm going out with Lucy on our first date. What does a date normally cost?"

"No more than twenty pounds, son," came the reply.

The following day the father asked, "Well, son. How much did your date with Lucy cost?"

"Just twenty pounds as you said, dad. It would have cost more but that was all the money she had!"

***

"Mum, what are prayers?"

"They are messages we send to heaven."

"Well, is that why we pray at bedtime, because the rates are cheaper?"

***

The Scot went down to London for an England versus Scotland match. When he returned one of his pals asked him if it was a big gate at Wembley?

"It certainly was," he replied. "One of the biggest I've ever had to climb over."

***

Hamish and his wife were standing in front of a women's clothes shop in Inverness.

"So, you really love that red dress, dear?"

"Oh aye," she replied. "It's a bonny dress."

"So you really adore that dress?"

"It's just ma size and colour."

"Okay. You know what, dear. Tomorrow we'll come and you can see it again."

The Scottish private was strolling across the parade ground when he was accosted by someone of the officer class.

"Soldier! Do you have change of a pound?"

"Sure, pal."

The officer turned red. "That is no way to address a superior officer you horrible little Scottish person! Now, let's try again. Soldier! Do you have change of a pound?"

"No, sur!"